SOS SA

TRAPPED

Enter If You Dare

Edited By Allie Jones

First published in Great Britain in 2021 by:

Young Writers
Remus House
Coltsfoot Drive
Peterborough
PE2 9BF
Telephone: 01733 890066
Website: www.youngwriters.co.uk

Printed and bound in the UK by BookPrintingUK
Website: www.bookprintinguk.com
YB0458E

FOREWORD

IF YOU FIND YOU'RE GETTING BORED OF READING THE SAME OLD THING ALL THE TIME, YOU'VE COME TO THE RIGHT BOOK. THIS ANTHOLOGY IS HERE TO BREAK YOU OUT OF YOUR READING RUT AND GIVE YOU GRIPPING ADVENTURES, TALES OF SUSPENSE AND IMAGINATIVE WRITING GALORE!

We challenged secondary school students to craft a story in just 100 words. In this third installment of our SOS Sagas, their mission was to write on the theme of 'Trapped'. They were encouraged to think beyond their first instincts and explore deeper into the theme. The result is a variety of styles and genres and, as well as some classic tales of physical entrapment, inside these pages you may find characters trapped in relationships, struggling with mental health issues, or even characters who are the ones doing the trapping.

Here at Young Writers it's our aim to inspire the next generation and instill in them a love of creative writing, and what better way than to see their work in print? The imagination and skill within these pages are proof that we might just be achieving that aim! Well done to each of these fantastic authors.

CONTENTS

Lillie Barnett (13)	69
Klarissa Buthi (11)	70
Aadit Shankar (11)	71
Megan Durham (12)	72
Isabelle Bonham (12)	73
Jessica Tite (14)	74
Millie Carnall (11)	75
Sophie Graham (13)	76
Lily-May Eudale (13)	77
Farun Church (11)	78
Arjun Singh Jhally (13)	79
Manal Faizal (12)	80
Fathima Ibrahim (12)	81
Jake Slorach (13)	82
Trinity Adeniyi (13)	83
Seynab Dahir (11)	84
Loretta Fortune (13)	85
Adwita Shukla (11)	86
Emily Eden (12)	87
Shannon Leonard-Day (14)	88
Sanvi Patel (12)	89
Indigo Wright (12)	90
Reece Perkins (13)	91
Sacha Kraev (11)	92
Anna Batchelor	93
Carla Sanchez (11)	94
Charlie Cusack (12)	95
Lana Crabb (13)	96
Darcy Williams (12)	97
Charlotte Bell (11)	98
Charlie Hunt (14)	99
Matthew Stones (12)	100
Zachary King (14)	101
Sanja Blair (12)	102
Erin Cole (14)	103
Dante Albarus (13)	104
Gennaro Calleia (12)	105
Abi Puvaneswaran (15)	106
Ridika Islam (11)	107
Joshua Bandy	108
Dhaneesha Patel (14)	109

Fort Pitt Grammar School, Chatham

Ruby Jordan-Hunter (11)	110
Aimee Sibbons (11)	111
Freya Ford (12)	112
Daisy Nye (12)	113
Ike Mosuro (12)	114
Emma Townsend (11)	115
Zoe Nwisi (12)	116
Ashrithaa Reddy Burugupally (11)	117
Daizy Carter (12)	118
Poppy Reynolds (12)	119
Morgana Davison (12)	120
Maia Turner (12)	121
Amelia-Grace Tomlin (11)	122
Megan Moth (11)	123
Libby Popov (12)	124
Bethany Hanks (11)	125
Elizabeth Grace Rye (12)	126
Sofia Basso (13)	127
Lillie Bilsby (11)	128
Amaoge Okoli (12)	129
Maisie Russell-Singer (11)	130
Orla Murphy (12)	131
Lilly Marley (11)	132
Darcey Nunn (12)	133
Orla Nixon (13)	134
Chloe Morris (13)	135
Lucy Thomas (12)	136
Tayla Gentle (12)	137
Emma Dorrell (11)	138
Brooke Turner (12)	139
Bernice Osa (12)	140
Olivia Dolley (12)	141
Hannah Teeton (11)	142
Layla Kearns (11)	143
Lucy Blackman (13)	144
Lorna Oloyede (12)	145
Isabella Seare (12)	146

Heath Park School, Wolverhampton

Rachel Harrison	147
Harkirat Chahal	148
Gita Plieskyte (11)	149
Maya Linton	150
Lola Richards	151
Alesha Hohm (12)	152
Leah Clarke (14)	153
Harmanjeet Ghuman	154
Aaron Ahir	155
Hugo Valencia	156
George Muchamore-Knight	157
Francene Tan	158
Abdullah Amedi (11)	159
Phoebe Botfield (11)	160
Dylan Moore	161
Diwan Ali (12)	162
Zofia Smolak (11)	163
Maya Kaminska (11)	164
Noor Ali (12)	165
Diya Grewal	166
Kristers Belakovs (12)	167
Katya Troath (12)	168
Gurbinder Ghalli (13)	169
Scarlet Bennett (11)	170
Vynxnt Jericho Melo (11)	171
Freddie Neale (11)	172
Sukhdeep Mann	173
Kayden Hines (11)	174
Alannah Miles (12)	175
Prachi Joshi	176
Mia Lau (11)	177
Kaira Lewis	178
Keira Swatman	179
Lania Salah (13)	180
Darrell Nyamunda (12)	181
Tanish Kaushal	182
Haya Rhuma	183
Ryan Hawkins (12)	184
Paula Reinfelde	185
Lilly Goodwin	186
Esha Bhakar	187
Shadi Damree (11)	188
Rares Ignatescu	189
Georgina Corbett (12)	190
Josh Butler (11)	191
Leah Blakemore	192
Kieran	193
Mohamed Amin-Mahamed (11)	194
Georgia Knowles (12)	195
Omed Hamid Hassan (11)	196
Davina Thomas	197
William Robinson (13)	198

Kirk Balk Academy, Hoyland

Holly Hopkinson (11)	199
Lucy Armer (11)	200
Olivia Haigh (11)	201

Minsthorpe Community College, South Elmsall

Oliver Hancock (11)	202
Tegan Gladys Lynne Patton (13)	203

St George's School, Harpenden

Lucy Evans (17)	204
Olivia McPhillips (12)	205
Catherine Kola-Balogun (15)	206
Max Soothill (11)	207
Jasmine Lota (13)	208
Alexander Russell (14)	209
Alex Falconer (13)	210

THE STORIES

Trapped

We don't have long. Time and oxygen is running out. We need to get out. We scream, "Help!" but no one hears us. We are stuck in a sinkhole, what can we do?

"Call someone."

"How? There's no signal."

"Oh this is not going great."

"I need to call my mum, I need to apologise to her."

"Why?" asked Lucy.

"She told me not to come here, she told me to stay home but I didn't listen."

"Wait, shush, I hear something!"

"Help!"

They're gone and we're stuck down here and we'll die in 22 hours with limited oxygen...

Atiya Perveen (14)
Denbigh School, Shenley Church End

Trapped In A Game

"You can't hide from us for long," the intercom blared out. Leah kept running while ignoring the intercom. "I need to get out of this game, I shouldn't have agreed to this," whispered Leah to herself. "If I get to the gate and wait for the dogs to sniff me out I can escape," planned Leah.
One week before...
"You're gonna have to do this game with me, please Leah!" her friend asked her.
"What if yo-"
"No, no what ifs, we'll both get into the game, promise," interrupted Leah's friend Mia...
"Mia broke her promise!" whispered Leah.

Lucy Effemey (13)
Denbigh School, Shenley Church End

Crushed

Darkness. Am I dead? Pain. No, alive. Crushing, squashing, annihilating pressure all over my body. Can't move, breathless, struggling to breathe, slipping in and out of consciousness. Stay awake, stay awake, stay... be*ep, beep, beep*, my mind slowly heaved itself back into focus as though it was being dragged through quicksand. Groggy, disorientated, down is up and up is down. Where am I? *Beep, beep, beep!* Flashing images, jumbled, tumbled memories. Falling, hurtling down, then nothing, just the crushing darkness. Noises from somewhere behind me, or was it above me? Light. They reach for me... Safe. Avalanche transmitter worked.

Catherine Murray (12)
Denbigh School, Shenley Church End

The Outcome

My head was in pain, my body wouldn't move. A shadow went over me and its gruesome smile showed its ruined yellow teeth. I just lay there broken.

"It's alright, you're safe," it said, while more chains attached to my body, the end of them were in the dark so I didn't know what they were.

"Who are you?" I stuttered.

It laughed at my face and my body grew weaker. "You don't know?" it glared at me. "I'm Fame."

"Stop this!"

"You signed the contract, this is your fault. Now!" It grabbed my head. "Let's begin shall we?"

Elsa Aspinwall (14)
Denbigh School, Shenley Church End

The Never-Ending Trap

"Run, but you'll never find an exit, you're trapped."
Wally gulped. "Camila," he said, pulling at his sleeve, "are you sure about this?"
"Yeah of course, it's safe," she replied. She walked to the corner of the corridor and let out her loudest scream as she fell to the ground.
"Camila! Camila!" he shouted. He clenched his fists, Camila stood up and reached for her dagger, a spark of lightning shot out his hand, pushing Camila back on the floor. A voice shouted from behind Wally, "Come in here if you want to live..." He reached for the door...

Odivwri (11)
Denbigh School, Shenley Church End

Trapped

I woke up in complete darkness. "Hello, is anyone there?" I said feebly. My throat was dry, like I hadn't had water in days. *Where am I?* I thought to myself. My eyes slowly got adjusted to the light. Looking around I saw machines around me, dangerous machines. Suddenly, I heard loud knocking from somewhere. *What's happening?* I thought, breathing heavily. Above me, I heard running and faster knocking. *Crash!* A loud sound rang through the room. People who I couldn't understand talking loudly and stomping around. Behind me a door opened and a bright light lit up the room.

Catherine Poovathingal (14)
Denbigh School, Shenley Church End

The Lost Incident

They're watching, they always have been. All-seeing. I don't know how long I've been here, I've lost track of time. I know I'm never safe, at least there's one hour, the recharge hour. I don't know what happens, everything just stops. The all-seeing stop looking. The unbearable training stops. It's the only time I get food. It drops from a hatch, just bread and water, they don't care if I survive. I don't know if there's more like me, but right now there's more training. Suddenly, the lights go out, there's shouting outside. The iron door creaks open...

Jamie Leroux (11)
Denbigh School, Shenley Church End

A Long-Lost Nightmare

"Write a simple story, it's not that hard."
Complete lies, I thought. My mind was crowded with ideas which fell apart and became nothing more than grains of sand in the raging arid desert in my head. It hurt, it hurt to think. I was already exhausted from yesterday and its brutal attacks. The words of voices long forgotten crawled their way into my mind and ripped it apart, "Useless, unwanted, ugly..." They kept taunting me in an eerie chant.
"Miss?"
I snapped back to reality to see my therapist looking concerned. I nodded my head and began to write.

Weronika Pietrzak (14)
Denbigh School, Shenley Church End

The Battle Of Our Falling

The battle of Yorktown, 1781. You could see the enemy firing, hear the loading of guns, preparing for the mass killing. We could smell the gunpowder and the rotting of once-standing soldiers. We'd once tasted glory, now we tasted near-death experience. You would've felt it if you were there. They had us surrounded, our only fate was dishonour or death. No escape. I looked into their eyes and saw they shared our want. Freedom. We wanted to go home and forget that we're killing machines. Monsters.
Bang! Johnny fell next to me. My best friend and colleague. We were trapped!

N'dea Lambert (13)

Denbigh School, Shenley Church End

Trapped In A Dystopian World

We were all trapped, couldn't go outside, couldn't see friends. Trapped. All day inside, no outdoors, well it was unsafe anyway. All those forest fires swallowing the villages and the virus consuming people. You would die either way. The world was getting worse by the minute. The King was claiming all the riches, leaving us penniless. Food was scarce and extremely dangerous to get. The children were travelling by small vents to steal the bare minimum, just to feed them for one small meal. Risking their lives daily to keep themselves alive, trapped in this horrific dystopia of a world...

Izzi Brockbank (12)
Denbigh School, Shenley Church End

What Happens After 1,142 Days?

1,142 days I'd been here, with my nemesis Jake, in a virtual world fighting for a chance to go home. As soundless as we could be, we crawled towards the portal. I felt hope. Suddenly, Bates jumped from who knows where and started giggling. "I may not have got what I wanted, but at least you guys aren't human anymore!" he screamed.
Feeling confused, we both jumped into the portal. We were back on Earth, but not at home, at a cemetery. I scanned the place and saw mine and Jake's parents crying at graves. "I'm Bates, wanna play? Hehe!"

Jayda Acolatse (11)
Denbigh School, Shenley Church End

Ghostly Trapped

It happened at once. I was in my bed sleeping, unaware of Satan that entered my room. With one sinister stare, it threw an immense force upon me. My unconscious mind questioned with curiosity on who was doing this. Then it stopped. With a huge relief, I called myself paranoid and attempted to go back to sleep. Unfortunately, it hadn't finished just yet. The ghostly force came back at me with an enormous strength, disabling me from moving or screaming. A couple of minutes later, the paranormal beast instantaneously left my room just so it can return once again...

Madhulika Pochana (13)
Denbigh School, Shenley Church End

The Pathway

I had her right in the path of my walkway... Rumble, rumble, the pathway opened and the girl fell. Falling, her screaming faded into the darkness below. *Splosh!* She clambered out of the water and started crying. It was dark, dingy and wet. The second wave came, four scary bloodstained clowns popped out the wall and started dancing around her menacingly. "Aaargh!" The girl was grabbed and thrown into the air. Smoke filled the hole, when it cleared she was in the house, the last wave came, spiders shot out the walls and water flooded the floor, filling up...

Dylan Card (12)
Denbigh School, Shenley Church End

Cornered

I didn't mean to kill her. I just, well, lost control. Darkness surrounded me as words like "You're a murderer!" and "How could you?" appeared around me. My feet were glued to the cold, wet grass while I felt like I was being cornered by my guilty thoughts. My knees gave way and I fell to the ground. "God, I'm sorry!" I shouted into the night. "Please forgive me, please!" I begged and begged until I was unable to talk anymore. I started to cry. To this day my guilt still follows me. I feel trapped, like I'm cornered.

Runa Nelstrop
Denbigh School, Shenley Church End

Wooden Prison

Her piercing screams ripped through her throat as she pleaded to be released. Pounding her fists against her wooden prison, panic rose in her thoughts as her breathing shallowed. She didn't deserve to be confined to this fate. When there was no response she fell silent. Pricking her ears to listen for the slightest sound, she came to the horrible realisation that they were gone. The muffled voices were no longer taunting her. Everything was deathly silent. Closing her eyes, she accepted that she would never escape. Then a quiet tap came from the coffin beside hers...

Tamara Grigoriadou (14)
Denbigh School, Shenley Church End

Omniscient

342 years, that's how long I've been trapped. In a coffin. Did I die? I cannot recall what happened before. The only thing I remember is my name, Omniscient. Will I ever be free? No. Death is inevitable. You can't escape it. That is until my coffin suddenly opens. What did I see after my reincarnation? War, death, destruction. It will never change. The sins of man will never be forgotten. God must have spared me and given me another chance.
Someone's coming, a girl is running to me. She's talking, I open my mouth to reply but... she's dead.

Emem-Obong Bassey (13)
Denbigh School, Shenley Church End

Stuck

1,142 days I've been here. Breathless days. Only little to eat and drink. I'm trapped forever. No one knows I'm here, I have no phone, nothing except a little food and water. I feel like there's no more oxygen to breathe. My heart is thumping so loud. I can't even hear myself think anymore. I feel trapped, more trapped than I ever have before. I'm afraid I'll die in this exact spot, I'm afraid I'll never see anyone again. I'm afraid that if I don't scream loud enough, I'll never be able to experience the future ahead.

Imogen Routledge-Prior (12)

Denbigh School, Shenley Church End

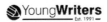
Trauma

I can't move. Able to hear cold, clinical instruments hurting me. Those who I knew turned their backs on me. Lying on the hospital bed trying to escape this never-ending nightmare. They're coming for me, planning to kill me. I can do nothing. Trapped, alone and stuck in trauma. A delicate flower withering by evil. Where can I go next? Not knowing what to do, my mind's racing with thoughts, making me restless. I can do nothing. Just falling in an endless deep abyss of nothingness. I don't know why. The Devil might have saved me in this summer breeze.

Kashvi Magodia (14)
Denbigh School, Shenley Church End

13th Madness

"It's the 13th today, hope this day goes well." I walked out the door and onto the road. There weren't any cars around, *that's strange*, I thought... until I woke up in a sweat still traumatised by what had happened. I checked the time and... it was the 13th. "Maybe it's just a nightmare?" Instead of going to school I came downstairs to see a pool of blood and... my mother in the middle of it. I collapsed. I woke up the next and... "No this can't be! It must be a mistake!" But it was the 13th...

Mansha Khan (12)
Denbigh School, Shenley Church End

Trapped

Only 30 seconds left until some UFO sucks me up on some stupid 'Serpents' Mound'. I don't know what these weird green bogeys are even doing on our planet! Oh no, here it comes... blackout. Wow! Holographic chains, sweet! Don't work properly though. Has a power switch, idiots. *Zwwoomm!* What was that? Bleep, bloop. A shiver goes up my spine, a slimy one, and it tickles. Argh! An alien! I brush my back against the wall and it dies. The door is open. I walk through. The alien aims his gun at me... *Bang! Bang!* I'm awake!

Sammi Rehman (11)
Denbigh School, Shenley Church End

Can't Run, Can't Hide

The lights shut off, dark as night, no one could see, the school disco was no more. Then a voice appeared, "You... can't... run... you... can't... hide..." It sounded like a scratched radio. Everyone was trembling with fear. I dashed out of the hall at this voice. Was this the school ghost everyone was making rumours about? Well, whatever it was, it was not good. I ran, turning left then right, left, right, then a dead end. The doors were locked, ghosts surrounded me with a cage. The voice was right. I couldn't run, I couldn't hide...

Martyna Pietrzak (12)
Denbigh School, Shenley Church End

The Voices

They are always there. Always looking at the world through my eyes. The voices in my head never go away. Not unless I do something, something truly horrible, but it gives me some peace, no voices controlling my thoughts and every movement. It's just silent, for that small time I'm not trapped in my head. So I head to the basement, the voices getting louder and louder. I open the door, grab the knife and sprint over to the skinny figure in the corner and bring the knife down. Blood's everywhere. But I don't care because finally there is silence.

Ellen Gibbons (14)
Denbigh School, Shenley Church End

Darkness

Running, panting, she had to go. Pushing leaves and vines out the way. The girl was tired and extremely worn out, but stopping was not an answer, for the monster of the darkness was upon her. Her friends, her family, her home was decimated, nothing was left. Well, it was her fault, this was probably some kind of cosmic karma. Then *crash*, she fell down a hole. Stumbling, the girl slapped onto the cold tunnel surface. The shadow, the darkness passed up above, leaving the girl in a puddle of her own tears. The girl who destroyed the world... Pandora!

Gabriel Moses (12)
Denbigh School, Shenley Church End

Cycle Of Time

I screamed in agony as the day repeated once again. Days... Weeks... Months... Years passed away as the day kept repeating again. My mentality dropping, driving me to the edge of my sanity. Eyes red, bloodshot from crying.
I woke up again, living through an endless cycle of night and day. I stood on a bridge looking at the radiant sun lose its bright lustre. My knees bent, getting ready to leap, then a voice softly whispered into my ear, goosebumps filling my body. As the words entered my ear, my eyes brightened once again, but this time with hope...

Sanjay Rajithakumar (13)
Denbigh School, Shenley Church End

The Graveyard

A nice sunny day turned into a gloomy night. I lived in a bungalow next to a graveyard. I'd always had a weird feeling about it.

One day, James and his friends dared me to go in there. I slowly entered, but before I could do anything the gate creaked open... "It's just the wind," I whispered, although I wasn't sure.

I slowly approached the graves, as I walked I could see the trees all old and with barely any leaves. Suddenly, I felt something grab my leg... it was pulling me towards its coffin! Then two more pulled me...

Rayyan Mohammed (12)

Denbigh School, Shenley Church End

Trapped

I lay on the cold, hard floor with my hand on my wound, trying to stop the blood from bleeding out.

"I'm so sorry."

I see her sat on top of me, crying her eyes out. I chuckle weakly. "We both knew that I'd take a bullet for you," I whisper. "And that you wouldn't do the same..."

"No! No! No!" she screams.

"I just never thought..." I said as I try to sit up. More and more blood starts to or out. "I never thought that you'd be the one... to pull the trigger."

Riya Nepali (11)
Denbigh School, Shenley Church End

The Castle By The Sea

I had visited the castle before. Vast and grand, it never failed to intrigue me. I ran, azure waves and coarse sand licking at my heels. There it was, basking in its own splendour. Majestic yet foreboding. Mysterious, yet it held answers. Suddenly, I noticed a trapdoor. Venturing through, I saw what looked like dungeons. Then, a hoarse voice sounded. I darted to the source, a man whose face I vaguely remembered. Our gaze met and I realised who it was. Stunned, I started to back away. I broke into a run as raindrops fell. Could it be… my father…?

Meera Batakurki (11)
Denbigh School, Shenley Church End

Hiding In The Shadows

Perfect. It has seemed to have lost its meaning over time. Perfect is just an act, our life is one big play, the reason is simple - fear. Fear of being eliminated, *game over!* No replays and no mercy. It's because those in power are scared, scared of anything less than perfect. So they will kill us off one by one, just for perfection. So we must hide for however long we need, but we'll always be here, watching, adapting, listening. We haven't done it yet, but know this; one day, however long it takes, we will win in the shadows!

Mia Gates (12)
Denbigh School, Shenley Church End

Spirits In The Darkness

"We are watching, we always are." The children screaming and crying was music to my ears. Pleasure filled my body knowing the children were suffering. Joy ran through me, my plan was finally successful. People call me crazy for my tormenting ways, to me I think it's creative and addictive. It feels as if something or someone is taking control of my body, which causes me to be so psychotic, yet I show no remorse. Not one part of me pities those kids, in that case why should I stop? It's the only thing that causes me pure enjoyment.

Lillie-Mae Planner (13)

Denbigh School, Shenley Church End

Zombie Apocalypse

The lift stopped suddenly, I was trapped! Cries of the zombies came from outside. Their arms crawled through the metal doors. The lift dropped, causing zombies to get crushed. *Bash!* The lift hit against the bottom floor but there were more of them rushing over to break in! The ones left at the top leapt down, one by one the glass slowly shattered. Their red eyes stared at me ready to kill. The glass was cracking slowly but surely. The metal door was opening with a loud creak. The glass shattered, the door opened. The zombies had got in...

Harry Lynch (11)
Denbigh School, Shenley Church End

Beyond The Gates

"What is the need for gates if nothing goes beyond it?" I asked Rae. She shrugged, we were at the park on the outskirts of town. There were huge metal gates that protected the town. Some said, it was an abandoned graveyard but I never believed it.

Suddenly, a ball flew over the gate. Curiosity took the better of us. We climbed over the gate to return the ball to the "person". When we got to the other side, everything went black! I waved my hand vigorously trying to reach the gate but then, a strong hand grabbed my mouth.

Titilayo Faluyi (11)
Denbigh School, Shenley Church End

Unknown

Don't ask me any questions, I don't know where I am, who I am or why I'm here. All I know is (and trust me I've tried) there is no getting out, alive at least! I haven't seen anyone in... forever. I don't even know if anyone exists anymore. *Boom!* What was that? I guess I'll find out, got nothing to lose.

I ran to the noise and I found something wonderful - a huge hole in the wall! All I could hear was fighting in the background, yet my mind was so tranquil. I could escape. I *would* escape!

Sienna Gleadall (11)
Denbigh School, Shenley Church End

Moon Man

Even if I could it would be futile to leave this crater-filled planet now. I can only calculate exactly when my next supplies will come. Can't play football without neutrons, nor basketball either. Chess requires two people too, and I'm not crazy just yet. I brought a computer but I could spend days trying just to get a single bar 'cause the satellites keep playing up. They usually send two people, not this time, just me. They said it would be just a year but, I only see mission extensions on the horizon. How long must I wait here?

Edward Williamson (14)

Denbigh School, Shenley Church End

Trapped

Strolling through the town on a warm, lifeless day, I stumbled across another missing child poster put up yesterday. As I was observing the poster I heard a shop bell, it was called 'Anthony's Doll Shop', but it was dark. I peered through the window seeing a doll that looked like me on the table standing there. Wandering in, I tried to grab the doll, but it vanished! It appeared on the highest shelf of the shop. I climbed the worn couch to reach it, suddenly I was on the shelf! Dolls were staring at me... Dolls were the children!

Jaina Jethwa (12)
Denbigh School, Shenley Church End

The Exam

"You may start your test," laughed the English teacher. Suddenly, the whole school collapsed. The sun had exploded and little meteors were flying to Earth. One of them hit the school. People were screaming, sirens were blaring and the fire was spreading. I managed to get into the hallway, but I saw something strange: a four-armed shadow standing tall, slowly walking to me. The creature came into vision. It was a molten monster, dripping with lava. I turned around to run, but there was another one behind me. I was trapped...

Aqibur Rahman (13)
Denbigh School, Shenley Church End

No Air

Why are there gates if there's nothing out there? The water is slowly filling towards the ceiling of this damned airport, and there's no way out. It was meant to be a summer getaway to Malago, Spain, but it turned into a summer disaster. Dead bodies are floating around this flooded airport and I fear that I will be the next. I start to scream but realise that I'm losing breaths and there's not enough air to get back. I find myself underwater and everything's starting to get blurry. I get back to the top and breathe...

Joseph Bradstock (13)
Denbigh School, Shenley Church End

Trapped In A Zombie Apocalypse

They search for me, the smell of my fresh brains excites them every second. My heart's pounding, my legs hurt after hugging them tightly. Sweat is running down my face. The zombies strolled around like mental people searching for something. They strain their ears to hear my heartbeat. The face of the zombie closest to me lights up with happiness. Its monstrous face faces me and strolls faster. My life jumps out of me and comes back. I start to shiver head to toe. I have nowhere to go. I'm stuck. Eventually, the zombie finds me...

Lishanth Sureshkumar (13)
Denbigh School, Shenley Church End

In A Dreaded Coma

1,142 days I've been here, stuck in this hospital bed, just lying here not knowing what's around me. I can't move, I can't see anything. I can't feel the world around me. How much longer will I have to stay here? This feels like a never-ending nightmare, imagine if I woke up right now, no one would care. My name is Lucas and I have lived five years with no parents, no friends or anyone to care.
Suddenly, I hear a beep and my eyes flicker open. I'm awake. Out of nowhere the door opens and I'm now trapped!

Sarah-Louise Day (12)
Denbigh School, Shenley Church End

Prisoners In Our Home!

Bang! The door shut. Windows locked. No one in, no one out. Prisoners in our own homes. Week in week out, no one to talk to, no one to see. The long lonely days felt like the hands of time had stood still. Days turned into weeks, weeks turned into months, and we still were trapped like caged animals in a zoo!

Gradually we are released but time is limited and we must stay away from other humans.

News flash! Second wave approaching, stay home! How many more lives will be lost during this global pandemic? COVID-19 2020.

Thalia Makris (11)
Denbigh School, Shenley Church End

Trapped

I was trapped in the third-class part of the ship while it was slowly sinking. The power turned off, I heard the creaking of the watertight doors opening, then all the doors unlocked. The ship was so dark I didn't know where I was going, then I started to feel water touching my feet and heard the sound of the waves splashing onto the ship. I could see the windows submerging underwater from the inside as the ship slowly flooded so I had to figure out how I'm meant to escape since I'm trapped on the bottom deck of the ship...

Rohan Spriddle (13)
Denbigh School, Shenley Church End

My Fake Friend

An addiction to drugs. Tried to stop but couldn't. Tried going but it didn't help. I don't know what to do anymore. Life is useless. A waste of time. A lot of hassle for no reason. As soon as you mess up you can't go back. That's how life works. People tried to help me, but I pushed them away. I should have listened to them so I wouldn't be in this horrible place. When you go into this the darkness consumes you. It eats your soul. I'm trapped. I'm scared and nervous. In this place, you're all alone.

Marcos De Araujo (12)
Denbigh School, Shenley Church End

The Darkness

The room was dark. I started counting at a couple of hours, however it could have only been minutes. I heard footsteps but I couldn't decipher whether it was a male or female. How could I have been so stupid to get in a taxi without the guards? I knew they were there for my protection, but I didn't think anything like this would happen without them. That's when I heard a crash, maybe just maybe I had been found. The door to my 'room' swung open and I was looking down a shotgun barrel. Now there is just darkness...

Oscar O'Keefe (14)
Denbigh School, Shenley Church End

42

Trapped

Another day walking down the path of doom. You're probably thinking of a dark, cloudy road, but no. It was a bright sunny pathway surrounded by green grass and lots of people. That's the problem - people. A fear that might confuse everyone and, in all honesty, it confuses me too. Everywhere I go it feels like someone's watching me, judging me. Even if they aren't it's still a thought in my head, taking over all other ideas and plans, however much I tell myself it's not true. It feels like I'm... trapped.

Robyn White (13)
Denbigh School, Shenley Church End

The Haunted House On Avenly Street

Avenly was a happy place, but down the road where nobody goes was a house that sat alone. Night fell, the sky turned black. Nothing in sight, not a single bird, just the moon glistening through the clouds and heavy rain so cold you could freeze. The house looked abandoned and lifeless. The windows were broken and boarded up, as if what was inside was too terrible to see. The house lived under a constant shadow as if the sun kept reaching for the walls then shrank away. People said the house was haunted by the man who died there...

Christiana Daramola-Moses (13)
Denbigh School, Shenley Church End

The Day Of The Lift

The lift stopped suddenly... There was only 30 minutes until the lift exploded while I was in there! I started to panic and realised there was an alarm button, so I pressed it but nothing happened. I could hear the countdown, 20... 19... 18... I fell to the floor and started to cry. Then I realised I had my phone in my pocket. "Yay!" I shouted, calling someone in my contacts. They came straight away. Finally, I thought as a security guard came and rescued me from my prison. I was so relieved, I won't go there again!

Mia Plumbridge (12)
Denbigh School, Shenley Church End

Escape From The Chateau

Floorboards were creaking beneath my feet, creating a cacophony of noise. I had to leave this house, these weren't my real parents, as I had just been informed. I have been confined to this lonely, empty chateau for more than half my life. It may sound like a dream, like a fairy tale, but the truth is it's a nightmare knowing that 'insane' people had been caring for me. Knowing that I didn't belong here made my plan to escape more important than ever. I had begun to leave when the top of the stairs creaked...

Martha Jones (11)
Denbigh School, Shenley Church End

Caged

I look over at the tempting key beside the cage door. Nothing guarding it. It's within my reach, what's stopping me? I gulp. In one swift motion, I grab the key, unlock the door and leave. I am free! I'm no longer trapped! I quickly leave the musty old room and go outside. The air is clear and I am surrounded by a gorgeous meadow that goes on for miles. The happiness doesn't last forever though. Despite the beauty that surrounds me, one question looms in my mind. If I am free, why does it feel like I never left?

Charlotte Carey (14)
Denbigh School, Shenley Church End

Waking Up

Running through the rain, my vision became blurry. I needed to get home before the whole park was underwater. I started trekking up a hill, wanting to escape. No matter how hard I tried to climb, the hill got taller and taller. My hands felt like batter, the rain fell heavier and colder. Squealing like a pig, I screamed for help as hail the size of golf balls rained down. Just as I gained balance, I fell. I hit the water, disorientated. Adrenaline pumped through my veins but it was no use. As I drowned, I awoke... from a coma.

Richie Catumbela (12)
Denbigh School, Shenley Church End

No Escape

I do not know how I ended up here, trapped in this glass room. There's fog around me and light beaming through the clear glass. I don't know why I am here and who put me here. *Is this real? Is this a dream?* I think to myself. I hear footsteps echoing around me, from the corner of my eye I see a dark shadow-like figure coming towards me. I slowly and cautiously move backwards. The figure that is moving towards me gets faster. I don't know what to do. I'm in the corner of the room, helpless and small...

Satvika Sadineni (13)
Denbigh School, Shenley Church End

The Coma

I can't move, I can't speak, I can't even take a breath. I have been put on machines to breathe for me since I can't do it myself. Me and my family were in a horrible car wreck. My siblings and I were found fighting for our lives. I was more endangered. So far I've been here for five days since the accident. The rest of my family have been discharged. Doctors say I am getting worse and might not wake up ever again.

Ten days later there is still no progress. They decide to take me off the machines...

Katie Simpson (12)
Denbigh School, Shenley Church End

Grandma Needs A Wash!

Oopsie! I totally didn't push Granny down the stairs! She kept locking me in her laundry cupboard and I was fed up with it! I followed her down the stairs and folded her up like laundry and put her in the washing machine. I put some powder in and turned on the cycle, hoping to cleanse her horrible soul. I watched happily, I saw shreds of her purple flowered dress going round and round. When the cycle had finished I folded her up again and placed her in the laundry basket and covered her with clothes for Grandpa to find!

Emily Bunting (12)

Denbigh School, Shenley Church End

Trapped In My Mind

Shivering from the inside, my mouth glued shut, I try to scream but no one can hear me. I can't see or cry for help, I can only hear voices. I'm confined in my mind with only one vision; flashing lights and a loud bang. I don't know what to do, I'm so scared, I feel so many things move around me, but I can't move I'm so frightened I can barely breathe, but when I finally stop panicking machines start to go off and people run in. Then I finally understand, I'm in the hospital, trapped in a coma.

Shilah Campbell-Odaro (13)
Denbigh School, Shenley Church End

Escape

"Leave if you please. Stay if you dare," the voice had boomed the moment we were at the gate. We should have listened and we shouldn't have dared. Now me and my best friend stand here, the bodies of our friends strewn around us. It was their little game. Kill one of us off each night, no one's death the same. So who would be the last standing? The walls started moving and the oxygen started running out. I tried to move but it was too late for us. Living and leaving? Not an option if you're all dead.

Ella Worsley (12)
Denbigh School, Shenley Church End

Trapped In Reality

It's the 1950s and I'm a woman. I want to do so much but I'm expected to stay at home. I have dreams of becoming a doctor, but I'm not allowed by society or my partner.
I wake up one morning and I have a letter addressed to me. It reads: 'You have been accepted to the medical school of London'. I go to tell my partner and he says, "You are a woman! You aren't capable of being a doctor! Just do your job and stay at home like all women are meant to."
I am trapped and broken.

Lolamae Calandro (15)
Denbigh School, Shenley Church End

Trapped

My name's Darla and I'm trapped. I've been stuck in this room ever since I can remember. My room has no door to it, just a window, but it's 1,000 feet high and if I jump out I'd fall to my death. I once escaped on my eleventh birthday. However there's only one way out of here, called the Infinity Road. It seemed like I was walking for hours until the Master, who trapped me here, caught me and sent me back. My name is Darla and I am 13. I may never escape but that is something nobody knows...

Areesh Saqib (12)
Denbigh School, Shenley Church End

The Weretiger

"Run! All you need to do is run! But I will find you!" the weretiger roared, shaking Dylan to the core. Dylan ran endlessly, his heart pounding as everything around him crashed down. *This has to be a dream, it has to be!*
The weretiger caught up to him, his teeth bared as he bit down on the child's neck. Dylan screamed in agony. As blood trickled down his neck he found an opening and struggled free and dashed the way he had come. He still ran endlessly while the weretiger chased him forever!

Anya-Lyn Nash (13)
Denbigh School, Shenley Church End

Help!

Help! we scribbled on the walls in blood, arms poked through the barricades on the windows and doors. You could hear the drops of blood on the creaky floorboards as the dead's groans echoed through the hallways. Sudden screeches made our legs shake as the groans got louder, the barricades started to crack. Slowly we started to see the silhouettes of the deceased. As the groans got louder, I started to back up to the exit on the roof, I heard the last barricade crack... the door was locked. We were trapped!

Xander Styles (12)
Denbigh School, Shenley Church End

Running Away From Death

Only thirty seconds left until I would be controlled by the 'Death Dealer'. My body was frozen to the spot and my hands and legs were in chains. I felt my life being sucked away and I had lost hope until my body was struck with sudden strength. As quick as I could, I broke the chains and ran for my life. I kept on running, not looking back, hoping the 'Death Dealer' was not chasing me. Suddenly, my body dropped and I was losing breath. I was losing consciousness. I woke up and it was all a dream.

Thanush Devadasan (12)
Denbigh School, Shenley Church End

Twinning Town

102 people were only in my town, I didn't know why but everyone kept disappearing, it was strange, plus my brother had been missing for over a year and something I still did not know was how everyone kept disappearing. The streets were lonely and abandoned, but the shops were still open and I needed to get some food, so I walked cautiously down to the shops. As soon as I got out of the door I felt weak and I lost consciousness as I'd been hurt.

I finally woke up, but not at the shops, in a black room...

Angelina White (12)

Denbigh School, Shenley Church End

Trapped

Crash! Another accident. Police officers crowded around the scene. A girl of 12 lay critically injured in the remains of what was a car. They tried to save her but they couldn't. I had died physically, but not my soul. I am the girl who died in the crash, my soul hasn't died, it never will. No one can see or hear me. I'm invisible. I visit my family, my friends and the people who tried to save me. They grew up but I'm still stuck in a 12-year-old's body, invisible. I am trapped...

Evana Joseph (11)
Denbigh School, Shenley Church End

Trapped

"Why are there gates if there is nothing out there?" he asked, looking out upon the vast oak wood forests. It seemed like it was to protect us but it couldn't be for there was no sign of life for hundreds of years. The older wizards of the towns said it was to stop the dinosaurs from getting in, but I had never seen any. There were rumours that somebody had left the safety of the gates and was never seen again. Lots of our people thought it was for the dinosaurs, but no one knew for certain though...

James Chalmers (12)

Denbigh School, Shenley Church End

The Endless Box

25 days I had been here, stuck in this endless room. There was nothing here, just emptiness. It was so dark and cold. I felt so unsafe. I was trapped, no way out. Then a horrible squeaking noise roared out of the darkness. It was dreadful. I slowly moved towards the sound, wondering what it could be. The small, dark space I was in blocked me out from seeing what it was. I persisted moving forwards, trying to get to the source of the sound. I was so close, just a bit further. Then my feet lost the ground - Argh...!

Alex Shipley
Denbigh School, Shenley Church End

The Girl In The Dungeon

The subtle humming of her soft voice rang through my ears. Every time she sang it was a rhyme, always the same one. Her name was Catherine. The chains around my wrists burned my skin, we were always wearing the same rags and every minute in the dungeon was agonising. All ten of us in one small, claustrophobic room, with bars in front of every window and door. We'd been there for 184 days now and soon it was time for one of us to be released. We were all waiting for someone to come and take us away. Catherine.

Meadow Worswick (11)
Denbigh School, Shenley Church End

The Disaster

I couldn't move, I couldn't breathe, my voice was stuck somewhere in my throat. Before my eyes was a scene of disaster. I was all alone as the victim of this disaster. Trees fell down, the earth shook and everything vanished into thin air. All of a sudden, two huge waves of water approached me. Water filled my eyes, ears and nose. I was trapped and there was no way I could get out. It was dark underwater, the water stopped me from breathing. My soul became eager to escape my body and then I blacked out...

Iman Ahmad (14)
Denbigh School, Shenley Church End

Trapped

I'm trapped. It all started when the tide pulled me in. I was screaming for help, although everyone could see me struggling, no one cared enough to save me. I was falling deeper into the cold, mysterious, gloomy water. After slowly drifting away into the darkness, I gained enough strength to pull myself back to the top, until my stress and sadness began to weigh me back down. So I gave up because the pain was overbearing.

Depression is a painful struggle that no one should go through alone. Always help.

Courtney-Jade Ward (14)

Denbigh School, Shenley Church End

Trapped!

We were trapped, no food and no water. We didn't know how long we would be here for because they didn't seem like they were going to let us leave. We didn't do anything! Well, we didn't think that we had. Unless we just didn't realise what we might have done. We couldn't call for help as we had no service. So we had absolutely no idea about what to do or how to get help. We hadn't eaten for days, was this the end? Was this where we were going to die? Was this really the end for us...?

Toyah Lewis (12)
Denbigh School, Shenley Church End

The Island

I was sweating, the waves were too high to swim away and they were coming. I backed against a wall and I quivered at their blood-curdling screams. The island, once tropic and majestic, was now torn apart with falling trees. I heard the heavy breathing of one of these creatures. I grabbed a rock and launched it at it. I missed and now they all knew where I was. Its foul green eyes glanced towards me and it cried, alerting its fellow zombies. A second passed, I thought I was safe. Then I saw them. I was trapped.

Maxwell Newman (12)
Denbigh School, Shenley Church End

Murderer

I am always watching, I always am. Like a hawk searching for prey but instead of prey, a way out. Any sign of weakness, I will try it. I need to escape, everyone's talking about it. Three days' time - my hanging. I wish the days were longer. There was one more way. Through the toilet...
It was tight, but I've done it. They think I'm fast asleep when I'm actually on the other side of those horrid fences. The public think murderer. I think greatest person in the world. I, am Al Capone.

Benjamin Guthrie (13)
Denbigh School, Shenley Church End

Poison Gas

I remember it, that fateful day. The day he found me. There's more of us now. He told us that if we could find a way out we were free. Only a few have managed it, others have died trying. A voice crackled through the speaker, the voice of him. He tells us all of his usual announcements, then says, "You will need to find a way out before the room fills with poisonous gas." This is our last chance, if we can't get out we are dead.
The gas starts seeping into the room. We need to move!

Lillie Barnett (13)
Denbigh School, Shenley Church End

Granny's Smoothie

Granny fell down the stairs. Oopsie! I totally didn't push her. I was fed up getting locked in the laundry cupboard so I folded her up and put her in the washing machine. I looked into the washing machine and saw Granny's eyes all mushy and bloody, after the washing machine was done, I poured her into a tall glass. I saw some teeth fall in too. After, I called Grandpa down so he could try my yummy smoothie. Grandpa loved it until he realised it was wife flavoured! It was Grandpa's turn next...

Klarissa Buthi (11)
Denbigh School, Shenley Church End

Trapped

2,500 days I have been trapped in here. I have been dying to get out. I am inside the storage room at Heathrow Airport. When everyone has left the airport it is very dark. When it's day I can't go out because of all the guards. Then I figure out a way to escape, there are cardboard boxes in front of the windows, I need to sneak behind the cardboard boxes and squeeze through the windows. Very surprisingly it actually works without any of the guards seeing me. Wow, I'm finally out of that place!

Aadit Shankar (11)
Denbigh School, Shenley Church End

Trapped In Your Own Mind Game

I'm trapped, trapped in my own body like I can't escape. Nothing I can do will make it any better. Everyone has that one person they can turn to if a boy breaks their heart or if someone makes them break down into tears. I used to have someone like that, she left me. She always had someone else she could turn to. She was my best friend and inside my head I was hers. But like I said, it was in my head. There's never enough room for me on the footpath. Nobody notices. How do I escape? Trapped.

Megan Durham (12)
Denbigh School, Shenley Church End

Can't Escape My Past

I will never know how I die or if I ever got a happy ending. Because I'm trapped. Trapped in my own past! I find myself back at the hardest decisions of my life. I'm in the corner just watching my past self, I want to reach out and tell myself no! But I have to face the past, I will never see myself happy again. It's the 22nd December and my life is about to melt in front of my eyes. It's bad enough knowing what will happen, but watching it's worse. It would be easier to say goodbye.

Isabelle Bonham (12)
Denbigh School, Shenley Church End

Trapped

Trapped. The cold lined silver walls that caged me allowed no escape. I felt beady eyes on my neck where my captor stared, keeping guard. I stood motionless, my heart pounding and sweat pouring down my face, still in shock about what I had just done. All that was left of the blood that flowed thick and scarlet in her veins was now staining my skin. It was only a matter of time until they came after me.

Suddenly, *bang!* The book shut and hit the floor as she fell into a deep peaceful sleep.

Jessica Tite (14)
Denbigh School, Shenley Church End

Trapped

One day, a group of three girls went to a haunted house thinking it would be a good idea to explore it. One of the girls said, "This reminds me of a horror movie!" The other two girls were hesitant to go inside but they eventually gave in. The oldest of the three was forced to go first, and as soon as she stepped inside the other two ended up standing by her side and two weak floorboards cracked and they fell to the Underworld. The three girls haven't been seen since, they were trapped...

Millie Carnall (11)
Denbigh School, Shenley Church End

In The Comfort Of Your Own Home

My eyes opened as the dark sky filled my vision. I couldn't feel my arms and my legs felt crushed. The last thing I remembered were the bombs, they fell from the sky and the sirens pierced my ears. I was stuck. Stuck under the rubble of my home, the one place I felt safe was killing me. As the dust and dirt filled my lungs I lost all hope. I was going to die. My life flashed before my eyes as the thought of my parents finding out crossed my mind. Suddenly, everything went numb. This was it. Death.

Sophie Graham (13)
Denbigh School, Shenley Church End

Trapped

All I could hear was the rusting and the clashing of the shackles on my hands and feet. I couldn't move. Suddenly, my kidnapper came and checked on me, but all I could see was a glimpse of sunlight from a crack in the barn door. He grabbed me and pulled me out of the barn. Then he put me into his car. *Bang!* The car door slammed, it woke me. He dragged me into this creepy, abandoned warehouse, where five guys in ski masks were waiting for us. He pushed me onto a chair, I was knocked out...

Lily-May Eudale (13)
Denbigh School, Shenley Church End

Gone

I am trapped. Dead but alive. I have all my senses yet I can't move. My family gathered around me, not knowing what I'm feeling. I want to reach out and tell them that I'm okay, but I can't because I'm trapped in a coma. Not being able to move is the most boring thing ever, I just wish I could wake up and see my family again. My friends must have missed me, I've been like this for months. I don't know how long it will be before I get out, but I want it to be soon. I hope!

Farun Church (11)
Denbigh School, Shenley Church End

Our Helpless Victims

We waited in the house, just us and no one else. An enticing notice placed prominently on the door. We waited and waited for our next helpless victim. This would be fun. As they opened the door and walked in we hid and waited. When they were not looking we grabbed one, then two and maybe even three. We took them to the basement and resumed our fun. Fun, fun, fun. We tortured them until they went limp, unable to scream or cry for help. We ended our pleasure and waited for our next helpless victims.

Arjun Singh Jhally (13)
Denbigh School, Shenley Church End

Death Is Near

There lived two boys, Ali and Nick. They both were hanging out in the park when all of a sudden it started to rain. They looked up at the sky and knew there was going to be a storm. They then took shelter and waited. Ali noticed a note. He picked it up and read it. 'Death is near'. He then heard it, a manly scream. He turned around to see Nick dead on the floor. *Oh no*, he thought, *I shouldn't have read it*. Next thing you know, he will be the victim. How could this be?

Manal Faizal (12)
Denbigh School, Shenley Church End

In A Room

I was feeling dizzier and dizzier, my head spinning so fast all I could see was a blur. An arm grabbed me, I wanted to scream but all of my energy was drained out. I woke up in this room, the atmosphere was eerie, it didn't feel right. Limping slightly, I ran to the door, pounding it with my fists. It was jammed. My hands were numb and white, glowing like stars in the dark. My hair was a bird's nest. I tried, I really tried. The cold sent a shiver up my spine. I was trapped and terrified.

Fathima Ibrahim (12)
Denbigh School, Shenley Church End

Watching

We see with no eyes. We speak with no tongue. We are the monster under your bed. We are the figure in the corner of your eye. We are omnipresent. We are the shadows always listening, always close. We lurk in dark places, watching, waiting. We live in the place you never want to look. We are the voice of doubt in the back of your head. We watch you sleep. We take you in the night, you just wake up in a new place with no escape. Locked doors, barred windows, chains. And we can prove it. Wake up...

Jake Slorach (13)
Denbigh School, Shenley Church End

Inifinite Abyss

A dark abyss consuming me. I'm trapped in a box, I've been stuck in here for too long, my hands are cold and my head's unable to stay up. I have never thought what would happen if I rammed the wall, as I ram the wall I break through, then I think, this can't be real, I must be dreaming, all while falling into another box. I break through the next one and I fall till I have landed in another eerie box. I can't break free from the cycle, it's too late, the deed's done.

Trinity Adeniyi (13)
Denbigh School, Shenley Church End

Trapped In My Own Mind

Every day is like the other. I wish one day would be different, but that would only happen in my wildest dreams. I pray I can be free, I hope and pray one day I will escape my own conscience. I wish I could spread my wings and leave this dreadful place. Being trapped is the worst thing to ever happen to me. Day by day my confidence fades away, normally I don't think twice about doing something, now that's the only thing on my mind. I am trapped, I am trapped in my own stupid mind. Help!

Seynab Dahir (11)
Denbigh School, Shenley Church End

The Button

I tried to scream but my voice had gone. I tried to run but my legs were stuck. The lights were blinding me, the sounds of screams filled the room. Faces of people here before me haunted me in my sleep. There was one way out. One by one, we got put in this room, but I never thought it would get to be my turn. The button, the one way out. Ten buttons and only one of them opened the door, I couldn't take it anymore. I pressed one. Everything stopped. The room filled with water and I drowned.

Loretta Fortune (13)
Denbigh School, Shenley Church End

Trapped

I was in the middle of a forest, the trees towering over me, blocking my way. I went pushing and shoving all the plants out of the way towards a strange sound. It kept howling as though it was in pain. I carried on walking towards the sound but when I thought I had found it nothing was there. I heard it again coming from a different place, so I walked towards it. This happened multiple times as each time I came to a different spot nothing was there. Then I realised I was where I'd started!

Adwita Shukla (11)
Denbigh School, Shenley Church End

Trapped

I'm a boy but I'm trapped in a girl's body. I wish I wasn't so shy. I want to tell my parents, but I'm scared that they're going to judge me. What should I do? Will they not care? Will they still love me? I sit on the bed trembling in fear of what my family will say. Argh, what will they say?
I stand up and walk towards my bedroom door, the floorboards creak as I get closer and closer to the door, one step at a time. I stand in front of the handle and reach out...

Emily Eden (12)

Denbigh School, Shenley Church End

Gone

And everything was gone. I was abruptly awoken by the sound of my alarm. I flung my body out of bed and got ready for another dreary day at school. When I was there I felt trapped, the only thing to look forward to was seeing my friends. I rushed to school, forgetting to say bye. I went to school, the hours passed quickly for my benefit. It was time to go home through the eerie forest... I felt like I was being followed, I picked up my pace. Before I knew it, everything around me was gone!

Shannon Leonard-Day (14)
Denbigh School, Shenley Church End

Remember Me

I have been stuck in this soul-proof dungeon for many days. I hate him for what he has done to me. Lying on the cold, wet floor, crying. I know no one can save me. My throbbing blisters ache beneath me and, like I said, this dungeon is soul-proof. I am the bird that has fallen down the chimney. I am trapped, hoping to be released. I kick, claw and scream, but there is no way I can be heard from ten feet down. I sit there holding my breath until my eyes shoot open as I hear... *tap!*

Sanvi Patel (12)

Denbigh School, Shenley Church End

Prison Life

I sighed and thought what life would be like outside of prison. I am not guilty. People set me up, I'm now in here for the rest of my days. The amount of times I've been disrespected, I can't count that high. I was fifteen and I was set up. Apparently I murdered my friend. I still can't remember his name. I'm 34 now, I don't want to be here. I think life could be better. The other prisoners are big burly men and then there's me. I really wish I could escape...

Indigo Wright (12)
Denbigh School, Shenley Church End

Trapped

I couldn't move, I was in handcuffs stuck in a prison cell. I didn't believe my eyes, it felt like I was in the future! I knew I had to get out somehow, so I kept trying to think of ideas and then suddenly I had one! There was a loose panel on the floor, I lifted it up slowly, as it was very heavy. A few minutes later, I was getting somewhere. Hours later I ended up outside the prison, but I had no clue where I was. Then I saw the police officers who started chasing me. Trapped!

Reece Perkins (13)
Denbigh School, Shenley Church End

Gas

I've been here for 42 days now... In a poisonous gas chamber. They brought me here and threw me inside, turning on the gas. Then they left, leaving me in a dark, very dark, gassy room. I'm writing this with one hand, the right one, the other one is lying on the other side of the room. The disease in the gas rips your limbs off over time... Oh, and my legs too, ripped off. The floor is smudged in blood. After the legs comes the head... and today is the day. Time to say goodbye...

Sacha Kraev (11)
Denbigh School, Shenley Church End

Trapped In A Time Loop

I couldn't stand it anymore, having to relive the same day over and over again. Every day was the same; waking up in the same bed, wearing the same clothes, eating the same food. Yet there was nothing I could do about it. That's when I remembered how I had gotten into this. I had to get to the same point where the time loop had started. I ran to the river, I knew what to do. I wasn't going to let myself die this way. But the same events happened again. I was truly trapped.

Anna Batchelor
Denbigh School, Shenley Church End

Trapped

It all started on a cold and breezy day. My clock was beeping at 8am so I got up to go and meet my friends at the park. As we were playing on the swings we heard a noise. I walked, trying to follow the noise when suddenly we all got sucked into a strange, creepy room. It was pitch-black with clues all around. But none of them worked. I nudged the door hoping we would be free but nothing happened! We had no signal, we were trapped.
I woke up, panicking. It had been a nightmare!

Carla Sanchez (11)
Denbigh School, Shenley Church End

The Dream

1,142 days I've been here. Weird things have been happening, I don't know what's happening but I think I am in a dream. Darkness is creeping up again and there is no way I can stop it. This time it is strong and powerful, the wind is blowing and it is becoming dark. I have to get back to my stick house quick, the gremlins will be coming, they are horrible vicious creatures, the only thing they are scared of is the light. So I always carry a torch with me just in case...

Charlie Cusack (12)

Denbigh School, Shenley Church End

Darkness

It is dark. I am alone. Why am I here? Laughter engulfs the air. I am surrounded. I must hide. I'm running away from the laughter, but hit a wall. A cage wall. I am stuck here. Does anyone know I'm here? I'm here scratching and screaming, I pull at the bars, they do not budge. My heart is like rivers. Does anyone know I'm here? I want to scream but my throat is sore. I want to run but my body is stiff. Then a voice cuts through all the laughter. Darkness falls...

Lana Crabb (13)
Denbigh School, Shenley Church End

The Flames

The spell was cast, there was a huge bang and a circle of fire sprang up around the witch. She crumpled to the floor. She could vaguely hear people calling her name. It felt like she was drowning, she kicked her legs, struggled for breath and desperately tried to make it back to reality. More people ran over towards her, they tried to get through the flames to reach her but the fire was too strong. It slowly died down, but when they looked around she was nowhere in sight!

Darcy Williams (12)
Denbigh School, Shenley Church End

Trapped

It was like looking through a dark tunnel, I could see the light fading away. What felt like seconds but was probably longer, I awoke. There was a bright white light shining over me. I tried to move but the more I tried the harder it was. I had a light bulb moment, I was in some sort of hospital or lab. I looked down at my hands, they were chained to a bed. I looked at my feet, they were also chained to the bed. Without realising I was doing it, I let out a scream...

Charlotte Bell (11)
Denbigh School, Shenley Church End

Escape

I was trapped and couldn't find a way out. I had been searching for a way out for a long time now. Others had tried to escape but they all failed, but how could I escape? We are being watched constantly. We had been looking for a way out we found a few options but all seemed almost impossible. It was worth a try, anything was better than being trapped in this place. Finally, we put the final plan together, we made the final preparations. We were going to escape!

Charlie Hunt (14)

Denbigh School, Shenley Church End

Alone And Confined

My eyes opened but I saw nothing. I tried to move my legs but all I could feel was the sides of the box I was confined in. The air was thin. The box thinner. I managed to rip off part of the mossy wood that limited me. I poked my hand out, only to feel the dirt and grime surrounding me. It was at that moment I realised I was six feet under! My heart began to pound furiously as I struggled in fear of death. I slowly became tired. I knew it was no use. I was trapped.

Matthew Stones (12)
Denbigh School, Shenley Church End

I Couldn't Move

I was trapped in a cave which was full to the brim with dangerous animals which could kill me in a matter of seconds. As I ventured further in I found a bear along with several corpses on the floor. The bear saw me and my worried face alerted it to attack. As it charged I ran as fast as possible, but the bear was ten times faster. I tried everything but it looked like it was the end for me. My life was about to end at the hands of a bear. I couldn't move...

Zachary King (14)
Denbigh School, Shenley Church End

Caged!

I wake up to a bunch of screeching noises, actually I wake up in a cage! I expected to wake up in my bed with birds chirping. I look underneath the cage and there's lava! How do I get out of here? Oh wait there's a lock that says if you can crack the code a portal will appear...
Ching! 2021! The lock breaks and the cage opens. I start falling... *Whoosh!* I'm all of a sudden in my bed and Mum calls me to have breakfast!

Sanja Blair (12)
Denbigh School, Shenley Church End

Trapped Inside A Coma

Are you trapped?

No not physically but I am trapped in a coma.

How did you end up in a coma?

I was in a car crash. I just hope I can recover and see my family. I know comas take time to recover from and I know I will probably need therapy.

Suddenly I woke up from my coma. It felt so good, so I decided to get up from my hospital bed and go for a walk. The doctor caught me and said, "Well done for a speedy recovery!"

Erin Cole (14)

Denbigh School, Shenley Church End

Trapped!

I was trapped! The same terrible day kept repeating. I had seen my family die over and over. How could I possibly get out of this loop? I tried to stop it from happening but it went on and on. Eventually, I stopped trying. The pain was more than I could handle. A ray of hope struck me! This was the first loop where everything went soundly. The day went fine, I was relieved.

Suddenly, I woke up, it was just a bad dream. I had escaped.

Dante Albarus (13)
Denbigh School, Shenley Church End

Trapped

Two years ago I was sleeping on the top floor of a 5-star hotel when I was woken up by the sound of gunshots and people with guns banging on the doors until they were only three doors away! I ran into the bathroom and to my delight there was a vent. I climbed in with caution. I crawled to the bottom floor in the vent and got out. Then I ran to both exits of the building, they were wired with bombs. We were trapped!

Gennaro Calleia (12)
Denbigh School, Shenley Church End

Trapped Heart

Trapped heart... My heart is trapped inside a cage. My emotions are all trapped tightly. I can't cry, get angry or explain. My smile is hiding all my pain. This mask I have on is not me. I'm trapped. I smile whether I am happy or sad. Begging for mercy but in endless pain. No one knows how hard it is to hide behind a mask. Endless pain every day, every moment. Trapped deeply in my soul. Trapped...

Abi Puvaneswaran (15)
Denbigh School, Shenley Church End

Trapped

I woke up to find I was in a dark room, but I saw a red flash, maybe it was a security camera? I tried to investigate but I was handcuffed, then all my memories started coming back to me. My heart started to beat rapidly, why did I believe that the man had been lost? Even though my mind said danger I didn't listen to myself. What was I going to do? I was trapped and a victim in all this madness...

Ridika Islam (11)

Denbigh School, Shenley Church End

Trapped

I was trapped! Trapped in a small box in the middle of a soundproof room. All I could see was the darkness. I thought I could hear whispering in the box with me, but it was just me going crazy. There was one window on the wall of the box in front of me. It seemed as small as a pea. I could feel myself getting crazier as every second ticked by...

Joshua Bandy
Denbigh School, Shenley Church End

Under The Sea!

I couldn't move, the deep blue water surrounded me. As I began to slowly faint, the sea pushed me further and further to the seabed. I fell deeper and deeper underwater as I began to black out. All of a sudden, I felt a rush of energy flowing through me. As I lay on the seabed salty water filled my body as I died.

Dhaneesha Patel (14)
Denbigh School, Shenley Church End

Them

They're watching. They're always watching. I've been waiting. Waiting for my turn to be taken. Each day, one by one, my kin are cruelly snatched away from our confinement.

The pounding footsteps arrived once more, their merciless, sinister cackles echoing through the hallway. With each parting more petrifying than the last, we shrieked and barked, knowing what was to come. The massive hands reached down hastily, grasping me tightly under the arms, making me yelp. A gust of horrifying foreign smells invaded my senses. I winced. They exclaimed, laughing, "Aww, this is the cutest puppy I've ever seen!"

Ruby Jordan-Hunter (11)
Fort Pitt Grammar School, Chatham

Conformation

Wham! The ship crashed into an iceberg.

"You don't h-have to do this."

Samuel stuttered, "We're in this together, if you committed a felony I did so we need to destroy the conformation. Water gushed into the ship, Samuel rushed out, closing the door before Sadie could exit. "You're a witness, I'm not going to jail," Samuel explained. And with that he was nowhere to be seen. As water filled the ship's contents, Sadie kicked for the surface, holding her breath, making bubbles, kicking for the surface. But for how long? Suddenly, movement stopped and all was dark.

Aimee Sibbons (11)
Fort Pitt Grammar School, Chatham

Sleep Demon

Can't move, can't breathe, am I even alive? Yes, I can see, although I'd rather not. There's someone by the window. No, they're by the door. No, they're by the end of my bed. "Who are you, what do you want?" Blood-curdling screams ring in my ears. Make it stop. Make it stop. Please. Please.
Someone help me. They're right next to me. Help please. Tears stain my cheeks, I can't hear my breathing, I can't feel my heartbeat.
"Wake up, you're okay."
A tug on my arm brings me back to reality and all I see is you.

Freya Ford (12)
Fort Pitt Grammar School, Chatham

Surviving A Zombie Apocalypse (A Nightmare Becomes Real)

"Mayday! We're approaching a wormhole! Mayday!"
With the pungent aroma of smoke crawling up my nose - I awoke. I sat up on the dusty ground, puzzled with what I had visualised. Had I lost my mind? I turned to see a dark figure approaching, limping. Had a crew member survived? As I drew in a breath, the air smelt of a rotting creature. I realised that it was no human that I was seeing - it was a rotting corpse. Panic-stricken, I backed away... only to realise that there were hundreds of corpses. Then, *crash!* Suddenly, my whole world went dark...

Daisy Nye (12)
Fort Pitt Grammar School, Chatham

The Cult

They were surrounding me like tape around a murder scene.
I was paralysed with fear, my heart pounding, my body stick
still like an icicle. "Just trust us," they said, "it will be fun."
Their pointed hats shaped to perfection, their cloaks draped
to the muddy concrete, they mumbled words I couldn't
understand. It was as if I was being dragged into something.
It was now cold. I was bare. Even though they turned
around I could feel their eyes burning from the backs of
their heads, carving a skull in my heart. Hell gained a new
demon.

Ike Mosuro (12)
Fort Pitt Grammar School, Chatham

The Force Field

"You can leave." He said it like it was an option! They were trapped inside a strange force field and he tells them they can leave? There was 50 seconds left until, *bang!* Ron was gone! Rose knew that she had 40 seconds until she was gone too. Out like a light. 222 days she'd been there, but she felt like she could survive for longer. 5... 4... 3... 2... 1... *Bang!* Maybe not. Then his beady eyes shot at Rose in her cage. Her little heart beat harder than ever before! "What a cute little guinea pig you are!"

Emma Townsend (11)
Fort Pitt Grammar School, Chatham

Suspense

They were watching, they were always watching... They were supposed to be in here, not me. Down under, deep down under. We started it but they're going to finish it. Air was running out. I felt paralysed. Confined to such a minuscule space, trapped in my own skin. The moment when you know it's over... that feeling of emptiness, knowing you're never going to wake up. I heard them from every angle. No matter what I did, I could hear them echoing in my head. Over and over again. The last thing I'd ever hear. Trapped in my own coffin.

Zoe Nwisi (12)
Fort Pitt Grammar School, Chatham

Hell's Museum

1,142 days I've been here. Stuck in here. Each day a horrifying punishment. Today was the worst. Blood dripping down from old victims who tried to escape... but they got caught and destroyed. I can't escape, even if I try, every time I try to escape they give me a punishment. Today they took it too far, the previous one being created and displayed. It's going to be me next. I can't, I need to escape, I can't bear it. I walk through the doll-hanging corridor... they caught me. I don't want to be turned into a doll...

Ashrithaa Reddy Burugupally (11)
Fort Pitt Grammar School, Chatham

Thumping

It is coming, I'm done for. I took too long, that's it for me and you. The thought of being separated lingers in my mind, yet I have my own individual trouble. The thumping, the tapping, the stomps - they are getting louder, closer, quicker. We need to escape, get out, say our goodbyes. It is the end. It is coming, what do we do? I have to try and get this done or it is truly over for us. Oh no, it's here! She's back, quick hide!
"Urgh, I'm sorry Mum, I forgot to clean my room, don't ground me!"

Daizy Carter (12)
Fort Pitt Grammar School, Chatham

Dear Diary

Dear Diary,
He watches me every hour, every minute, every second.
There's no escape, I'm locked in a bedroom scared and
scarred. Footsteps come up the stairs. This is the worst part.
I watch the door creak open. A foot enters the room. Bruises
are created, but there's no escape unless...

Dear Diary,
Well, I am not trapped anymore. Pools of blood fill the room,
I kinda like it, it brings out some colour in the room. I am on
my way to see my parents. Finally. But first I must take my
daily five pills.

Poppy Reynolds (12)
Fort Pitt Grammar School, Chatham

Again?

This happened yesterday. I woke up at 7am and got ready for school. The only thing, it was a Saturday. I looked around and couldn't see anyone, strange. Suddenly, I was back in my bed, in the same position I woke up in yesterday. Confused, I stood up. I got ready for school, but surely today would be Sunday, right? My family was nowhere to be seen, maybe they were out? It was almost like I was trapped in time, the same day repeating.
To this day I haven't managed to free myself. I wonder what year it actually is...?

Morgana Davison (12)
Fort Pitt Grammar School, Chatham

Drowning In Thoughts

Silence, I'm bombarded with words, overwhelmed with thoughts. I put on music in an attempt to drown out the endless ringing in my head. But the meaning of the words cuts my heart, lengthening the crack that was already there. I rattle bars, I grapple at the ragged rope, heading on into nothingness - but sometimes holding on hurts more than letting go. My stomach is doing backflips inside my chest. I take a deep breath. I close my eyes. The worst prison of all isn't a cave, or a coffin. The worst prison of all is my mind.

Maia Turner (12)
Fort Pitt Grammar School, Chatham

The Last Five Minutes

There was only five minutes left on the dreaded timer. Oxygen was running out. There was no hope. I felt like giving up. I'd already been in here for 42 days. Nobody else was here except for me. I felt scared, lonely and depressed. I didn't know what to do. Suddenly the doors opened, and I saw light, my family, my friends. I sat up, realising I had been in a coma. I felt over the moon. After suffering the stress and sadness, it felt amazing to see other people and hear other voices again. After weeks, I felt happiness.

Amelia-Grace Tomlin (11)
Fort Pitt Grammar School, Chatham

The Creek

I never thought they would do this; prank me, yes, but this, no. I can't handle this, can't this be a bad dream? No, I'm not dreaming, this is real. Maybe it is and I'll wake up? No, very real. Should I run? No, won't work, plus if I try I'll just feel more pressure. But still, it wasn't my fault! How could I have been so stupid! "Meet us at the creek," they said. The popular kids never liked me and all of a sudden they want to meet me at the creek at midnight? And now, I'm trapped...

Megan Moth (11)
Fort Pitt Grammar School, Chatham

Should I Book?

She was scared for her life, the corridor was the same, the sign read *Intensive Care Unit*. She started running, still it repeated itself again and again. Suddenly, she stopped abruptly, there were people standing, staring. To her surprise she realised she knew them. It was her mother, father and two siblings. But it couldn't be, they all died in a house fire a year ago... It turned pitch-black, her eyes opened, she was once again in the care unit. I watch her repeatedly on the screen, tied to a theatre chair...

Libby Popov (12)
Fort Pitt Grammar School, Chatham

Apocalypse

"Arghh!" I heard another blood-curdling scream from the city of Carex.

"The zombies, they're here!" shouted an old man with grey hairs poking out of his chin. My mum and dad rushed me and my younger sister into a secret underground bunker. As I was climbing down the ladder, my dad ran back to our cat Tigs and Pops, our bird. Once we were all down there the earth started to shake viciously. We could hear screams coming from above ground, shrieks from every direction. Could this be the end?

Bethany Hanks (11)

Fort Pitt Grammar School, Chatham

Imprisoned

The rusty prison has been abandoned for well over a decade, its cobwebs have grown and dirt has collected. A thick layer of dust lies upon my index finger as I gently run it along the wall. I sit here slouched against the locker, all day and all night, unsure where to go next. I stay sitting here, frozen in unforgivable time for the 285th day of this year. I've been locked here for just over nine years, soon to be ten. "What happened?" you ask. Let's just say to always hand in your homework on time!

Elizabeth Grace Rye (12)
Fort Pitt Grammar School, Chatham

Cyclo

1,142 days in an endless cycle. My mind - black! Part of me hopes I never wake up, as I know the struggle I will encounter. All is peaceful in this blurry abyss. It feels like a weight has been prised off my shoulders. My problems evaporating. However, I realise when I wake these problems will flood my brain beyond a point of control. 1,142 days I have tried to break bad habits - to be the better man, but I can't. I try to resist the urge, the thirst that is ever growing, but it overwhelms me. Back to square one.

Sofia Basso (13)
Fort Pitt Grammar School, Chatham

The Lady

I froze... panting, nervous, no idea what... to say. The room went dark. My heart stopped beating. My brain went blank. I threw myself to the door, trying all I had left to open it. It wouldn't unlock... Shoving and thrusting, this way and that. I felt as if someone was cutting my throat. I was falling... falling... falling... Who was it? Who am I? Where am I? I stopped. A lady? Who is she? Something grabbed my arm, dragging me to the lift. The lady again. She turned and stared at me. A blood-curdling scream...

Lillie Bilsby (11)
Fort Pitt Grammar School, Chatham

The Lost Island

I'd been shipwrecked on an island. The lost island... I explored the island, as I got deeper into the forest, I heard screaming, a piercing scream. I fainted at the sound of the screaming.

When I awoke, there was a man in a hood and he told me to go in a cave, then he was gone. I walked in deeper, I found myself trapped. There was a box. I put my hands on the side and heard a click. I felt something like electricity running through me. I yelled as it engulfed me, I saw blue eyes, then disappeared...

Amaoge Okoli (12)
Fort Pitt Grammar School, Chatham

Ablaze!

I ran into the burning building. I had to save her. Smoke slipped down my throat, followed by a series of wheezing coughs. A chunk of burning rubble landed on my leg and I cried out in agony. My scalded leg was livid red. But I had to find her! The air was hardly oxygen anymore. I needed air and soon. I fell on my knees, eyes streaming and gasping violently. With a shuddering sob, I struggled to my feet. Blundered straight into her corpse. No time for grief. I numbly turned to the door, which was locked...

Maisie Russell-Singer (11)
Fort Pitt Grammar School, Chatham

Believe

How could they do this to me? Everyone is equal, they said. We got treated the same, they said. Yet here I sit. Behind bars. Locked away. Alone. I see them pass me. They point and laugh and sneer. Some even poke things at me. I do little to nothing all day but feel sorry for myself. What a way to live. I feel like an outcast. Unwanted. Unloved. Like I am a disappointment. I do not approve. They treat me like I'm an animal. How dare they think this? Oh, wait. That's because I'm a monkey.

Orla Murphy (12)

Fort Pitt Grammar School, Chatham

Trapped

Days I've been here, stuck here with no food or water. Blood drips down my face. My head starts to spin. I see a man. He walks towards me. I panic. *Bang!* It all goes black. I awake to a terrifying face looking down on me. I jump in fright. I sit up and bash my head. I am in a glass tank. I appear to be in a black dress with cracks on my face. "What do you want?" I say. No reply. I am so nervous, when *poof!* I'm a doll! "Come and play with me!"

Lilly Marley (11)
Fort Pitt Grammar School, Chatham

The Light

162 days I have been lying here. Me and my mind. No one to talk to. My thoughts go adrift sometimes, trapped with only my mind. Every day I stare up into the ceiling light of the hospital. I can't move or get up. My body numb and stiff. My screams echo throughout my head. Nobody can hear me, I'm alone. The doctors talk to me often, I can tell they are losing hope. Today is different, they all say bye and then it happens. Darkness takes over and I see a light at the end of the tunnel.

Darcey Nunn (12)
Fort Pitt Grammar School, Chatham

Lights, Camera, Action!

You would think it's like the perfect life, living in a movie. But, knowing they're all watching you, every step, every breath, no way out! Everybody knows me, my life. My story isn't very interesting when I'm scared to even get dressed in the morning, knowing they can see me! I am going crazy. Why me? Am I really that special? Many escapes have been attempted by me and previous stars. They say the eye is always watching, so when I escape, be careful. You could be next!

Orla Nixon (13)
Fort Pitt Grammar School, Chatham

Trapped

It's never easy, the guards constantly staring you down. I'm so trapped in prison, I don't even get privacy to sleep. I wasn't even the one who murdered Jack, the person who did is still out there now, god knows what he's doing. All day I sit here shivering, hungry, never knowing what is going to happen. I feel paralysed. One day I start thinking and all of a sudden I break out in sweat. I realise I am the one who killed Jack. I am the one who needs to be in prison.

Chloe Morris (13)

Fort Pitt Grammar School, Chatham

The Games

My forehead is sweating. My heart is racing. I am physically unable to move; every part of my body is trembling. The tally on my wall is too many to count; I'm sure I have lost count by now. "The games are over, you win, now let me out!" I somehow manage to bellow. The end seems near yet so far. Each day, hour or even minute could be my last. I don't even know my own name, let alone how I got here. I quickly realise the games are not over - they have only just begun.

Lucy Thomas (12)
Fort Pitt Grammar School, Chatham

Haunting Me

It was watching me, clearly amused by my attempts to escape. I clawed at the strange pink walls, although aware it would do nothing. Tears made my vision blurry, my sobs choking me. I think I know where I am, but I know who 'it' is. My energy is drained by my previous screams of dismay. Nothing will work. I'm stuck here alone, with it. I am in a never-ending nightmare. I don't want to see that ghost, I just wish I could get out of my brain. It's not helping me.

Tayla Gentle (12)
Fort Pitt Grammar School, Chatham

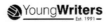
How Do I Escape?

The lift stopped suddenly. There was no way of escape! I felt it getting hotter as the metal walls came closer. I felt my heart skip a beat every five seconds. My breath got heavier as my oxygen was running low. In the far corner of the life, I noticed a small lever. I reached out to grab it but it was too far. There was no way of escape! I felt my eyes getting weaker as there was no oxygen left. How was I going to escape? My breath stopped. I was well and truly dead.

Emma Dorrell (11)
Fort Pitt Grammar School, Chatham

Silenced

Dead still nights, dead still mornings... eerie sort of but used to it, I am. There is one thing I long for more than life, to run in the long grass once again (hopefully my life will resume). Mentally trapped in my own thoughts. I am certainly not mentally insane, I am not one of them; or am I? This coma will persist my will to leave, I am sure of it. I haven't tried to talk to him yet, persuade him to let me go, be freed from my endless sleep. Silenced I was.

Brooke Turner (12)

Fort Pitt Grammar School, Chatham

Bondage

They are watching, they always are. Monitoring my every move, locking me away from the outside world, taking away my freedom, my rights as a human being. Oh how I despise them. It's dark in here, lonely and solitary; secluded. My life is no longer mine, it never was. I am being held captive and no one knows. The walls are damp from my tears, all I feel is pain and sorrow. My pleas go unheard and my tears go unnoticed. I am in bondage and there's no way out.

Bernice Osa (12)
Fort Pitt Grammar School, Chatham

Trapped

I was there for 1,142 days with no food and only a puddle of water. My skin was dry and scaly. Skinnier by the day and beaten. It was gloomy with blood-curdling noises! One day, I was dragged into the corner and started going down. Butterflies in my stomach as I was falling... Then I stopped. I squirmed around, I couldn't move, I was in an air-tight room filled with water. Time was running out, or so I thought. Because it was then I remembered I was a mermaid.

Olivia Dolley (12)

Fort Pitt Grammar School, Chatham

Buried Alive, Or Are You?

They are watching, they always are. You'd think that in the space of a coffin there's be no space for a camera. But in this place anything is possible. Every day there's a swoosh, followed by a scream that splits my ears open. I heard footsteps every day but today they got louder. There was a creaking noise and then my eyes were burnt as I was dragged to a white room and then scratch, scratch, scratch, and *whoosh*, the world went dark...

Hannah Teeton (11)
Fort Pitt Grammar School, Chatham

My Life Is In Your Hands (Don't Kill Me)

I can't take it anymore, it feels like I'm going to explode into a million pieces. My time is decreasing, I don't think I can take it for another day. Why? Why is he doing this to me? I can't process that he is trying to kill me. He keeps saying, "Do you need more food?" just to be kind and because I need to be looked after. But what he doesn't know is that I am a fish, if he keeps feeding me every day I am going to die!

Layla Kearns (11)
Fort Pitt Grammar School, Chatham

Future, My Future

Sat in a hall in rows, they watched over us and waited till one of us made a mistake. Any mistake and our lives would be ruined. The voices in my head, it was too much, I couldn't do this anymore. One noise and I would regret this. The clock moving faster and faster, just like my life, my heart, my *time!* They whispered in my ears, telling me that I was finished.

Finally, they took my exam paper away, me awaiting my future.

Lucy Blackman (13)

Fort Pitt Grammar School, Chatham

I Want To Know

They are watching, they are always watching. They won't tell us why, how or who, they won't let us in or out. We are trapped by walls and bars, held against our will. They say we are the last of human civilisation, but is it true? Our shouts and cries go unheard. They say outside is a wasteland. Although I don't believe, I want to see the real world. I want to escape from the fear, the hatred and the uncertainty. I want to know.

Lorna Oloyede (12)
Fort Pitt Grammar School, Chatham

Red Door, Yellow Door

As I gasped for fresh air, my sunken eyes blinked. I was left in a dark room. All I could think about was the two doors in the distance. One red, one yellow. Yet I couldn't move. How was I meant to escape? What were these two doors? Thoughts engulfed me, my breath echoing in the dark abyss. Red door. Yellow door. Red door. Yellow door.
Creak! A coldness crept up my spine. My limbs were stuck. I was trapped!

Isabella Seare (12)

Fort Pitt Grammar School, Chatham

Trapped

Dazed, Jess woke up in a hospital bed, 'huh?'
Wait, I'm handcuffed, she thought to herself. *What did I do? Anyone?*
Immediately, the lights dimmed and a chill shot down her spine. A strange sensation ran through her body, as if she was being watched.
Her dark eyes locked in on the right corner of the room... she could feel someone staring back. In that moment, she went into panic, somehow her voice was paralysed. Two slender ghost-like hands appeared either side of her gripping on to the bed. Pulling itself up, the figure revealed its face...

Rachel Harrison
Heath Park School, Wolverhampton

Paralysed?

Deeply I breathed, I was unsure of what was happening; there was nothing I could do. I couldn't speak let alone move. I could feel every single movement, the pain was agonising. My soul watched over my paralysed body. I was helpless, I didn't know what to do, they needed to know. I was trapped. My mind and emotions were screaming for help but nobody could hear me. The surgeons began the heart transplant, cutting deep into my chest which felt like thousands of knives being stabbed and twisted directly in my heart continuously. I needed to get help, *fast!*

Harkirat Chahal
Heath Park School, Wolverhampton

Trapped

"It's Thursday!" announced the radio. I spent an exhausting day at school. The next day I heard, "Thursday!" I thought nothing of it. The strange thing was I had the same lessons like yesterday. It was like I was trapped in the same day I took it to my advantage. I missed lessons, stayed out late and went to parties. Every morning I would hear, "It's Thursday!" so I would have to think of something new to do every day so I wouldn't be bored because I've done everything in the last couple of weeks Thursday has been repeated.

Gita Plieskyte (11)
Heath Park School, Wolverhampton

Trapped

I've always wanted to see myself from other people's perspective. I see myself as a great person just living a normal life, although it feels like every day something bad occurs; it always has something to do with me (I'm always blamed). Today I found out why. Finding groceries in the shop, I saw my favourite treat back in stock, it was a shame I didn't have enough money! I left until... My other side came. It snatched the sour sweets and *crash!* I jumped through the window feeling happiness but with tears pouring down. I was trapped with... me.

Maya Linton
Heath Park School, Wolverhampton

Trapped!

I can feel it again... my pale skin drenched with cold sweat, my skin crawling with anticipation. Every sound, every bellow around me is screaming inside my head. Why won't it all just go away? I feel rigid with fear, what is my next move? My bare feet teeter on the cold, smooth edge, my eyes burn with tears and the noise... the noise, inside my head's just getting louder! "Lola, Lola... *Lola!*" I open my eyes and glance frantically around me... I'm here again, stood shaking on a 4-inch piece of wood, 4 feet in the air. *Trapped!*

Lola Richards
Heath Park School, Wolverhampton

Forever Trapped

I was dashing home when a mysterious doll suddenly caught my attention. Curiosity got the best of me; I had to go inside. Figures on display were staring at me. Creepy! Simultaneously, they hissed, "Let us out." One of them stared through my soul. "Touch me," one chanted insistently. A hallucination popped into my head, showing what would happen if I dared touch the doll, but I couldn't resist; I had to get the itchy urge out of me. I felt a sharp pain, I stiffened; I felt weaker... I was stuck inside its interior, I... was... trapped...

Alesha Hohm (12)

Heath Park School, Wolverhampton

Trapped

Today was supposed to be just a normal day...

A small group of young adults approached me, each carrying leaflets in their hands. My initial thought was, *what are they selling?*

I kept my head down, hoping they'd just walk past but they grabbed me and said, "No point in being rebellious."

I didn't want to be in this predicament, but I had no choice. They grabbed me and pushed me into the back of a car. We arrived in their chosen destination soon after.

I was silent. I didn't speak once. Wherever we were, it was freezing...

Leah Clarke (14)
Heath Park School, Wolverhampton

Trapped In My Mind

Shockingly, I was still trapped. Imprisoned in my mind. Kidnapped by my past mistakes.

Everything wasn't supposed to be like this. She shouldn't have died. I shivered as I tried to stop the panic taking over me - I stood in front of her dead body, shaking.

It has been 5 years, but it glued to my mind like yesterday. I murdered her.

I knew she wanted revenge. She haunted me in every dream; appearing, always suddenly. Holding the same weapon I had, in the same terrifying way. Moonlight streamed through the jagged glass that had once been the window...

Harmanjeet Ghuman
Heath Park School, Wolverhampton

Trapped

Trapped, nowhere to hide. Nowhere to run.

Quietly, I lay consumed by the darkness. Tears streaming down my face. I could feel the towering walls beyond my reach. I ran my hand along the cold bricks, miniscule flakes slowly descended on a long journey to the ground. Life took a deep dive underwater where I drowned in self-hatred. I was trapped in my mind where the sounds of my family deafened me.

Suddenly the box moved, crushing my body. I couldn't open my mouth to scream.

"Help me!" I managed to whisper. My voice echoed.

All alone.

Aaron Ahir
Heath Park School, Wolverhampton

Trapped

I cried through the dry, iridescent mist. I realised I was in a dull room. No living soul, nothing around me. My weary steps faltered. I tried to touch the things around me. Nothing. I walked until I touched something. It was frigidly cold. Suddenly, it disappeared. The object I was touching dissipated. I got it off my mind and trotted on. I sauntered around and found a door. Just a simple wooden door. I blew on the dusty passage and I saw the word 'Exit'. I opened the door and breathed in the sweet, fresh air. I pondered, "Freedom."

Hugo Valencia
Heath Park School, Wolverhampton

Springlocked

As the moon rises, the numbers 12pm appear: the night shift just began... At around 3am I had an urge to explore. I then found a room saying 'parts and service'. "Argh!" *A scream*, I thought. A child's scream getting louder; more screams were heard. I found a suit I put it on... I saw souls of dead children. All of a sudden, I screamed the springlocks engaged, killing me...

I was trapped in the suit, I have been thinking, *how long has it been?* The door creaked open, I heard whispering, "30 years."

George Muchamore-Knight
Heath Park School, Wolverhampton

Inception

I hear it calling my name. I run to the endless void of nothingness. Running as if my life depends on it, but nothing comes. Everywhere I look, I see myself. Lost. All this emptiness spreads through my veins; I can't breathe here. I run myself into the wall opposite to me, only to be back where I began.

I'm dreaming a dream every night. Again, my dream is renewed.

I see them. Watching. I'm still here, it's only me. This inception is carved in me, I'm trapped, this life of lies. This inception is slowly killing me. This inception.

Francene Tan
Heath Park School, Wolverhampton

Trapped

Standing up, he looked at darkness. "What is this place?" he said. Confused, he started looking around. All of a sudden, a dark shadow stepped out. Terrified, the boy ran.

"You can't run from me little one," said the voice. "Come to me and no harm will be done to you." The boy stepped forward.

The next thing he knew, he was in a room. "Are you okay?" The boy nodded. The figure, who was a lady, got out a device and gave it to the boy. "You are trapped in a world, where you die or escape..."

Abdullah Amedi (11)
Heath Park School, Wolverhampton

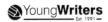
Trapped...

It was 5:31pm. Mom was cooking dinner, or so I thought. It had been an hour; I had started getting hungrier.
My parents were arguing, my name kept being mentioned. Suddenly Mom came running up the stairs calling my name. I dashed to my door and locked it, trapped. I didn't know what she wanted but I knew it wasn't for a good reason.
The only thing I could hear was my fear-filled breathing. The handle was moving...
Smash! I hid. She had got in. I'm going to die, aren't I? My body was full of anxiety...
"Help me!"

Phoebe Botfield (11)
Heath Park School, Wolverhampton

Trapped

Slowly, I opened my eyes to a cover of darkness. I couldn't move; I felt like I was superglued to an electric chair; I didn't know where I was... I was shrouded in a bed of earth. I panicked... I couldn't breathe; bits of earth dropped in my mouth as I gasped for air! Ugh! I felt something crawling up my arm while trying to work out what the creature was. It started to crawl up my neck and I was petrified. I couldn't move, I couldn't breathe, I couldn't see, whilst the creature crawled in my mouth... *Argh!*

Dylan Moore

Heath Park School, Wolverhampton

The Back Rooms

Where am I, I woke up today in this weird place that feels oddly familiar. It's all empty. It has old yellow wallpaper with a rough carpet and flickering lights and humming that sounds like an AC but it's still room temperature and no vents.

I have been walking around for hours walking into different rooms, the rooms have different shapes but are all the same. This place goes on forever I have lost all track of time. I have been in here for 10 days.

Day 15, someone no something is here, I'm not alone. Please help me.

Diwan Ali (12)
Heath Park School, Wolverhampton

Trapped

The numb wind crawled up my tensed body. Questions were chanting inside my head: *where am I? Who took me? Is this a dream? Bang!* The door flung open, I could see two red eyes, I felt like they were venom-like. *Cling!* A lightbulb lit up, it was yellow, around the room all I could see was bags on the floor. I looked at the creature. Its robes had rips and stitches; its teeth were sharp. The ropes itched me. Suddenly, the anonymous creature was close to me. And that is the last thing my traumatised memory can remember.

Zofia Smolak (11)
Heath Park School, Wolverhampton

Trapped

Running like there is no tomorrow, I grab the nearest weapon I can find and run out the smashed kitchen window. My phone is pinging, missed calls, unread messages but there is no time to waste. I hide behind some abandoned houses breathless, losing more hope. I can smell the cologne from 4 meters away. My mind is overthinking what will happen next. The scent is slowly coming closer every second. My body feels paralysed but I need to run faster than my body has ever run. Memories flood me as the unknown person pulls down his mask...

Maya Kaminska (11)
Heath Park School, Wolverhampton

Trapped

Running away as fast as a cheetah, I entered a house. Without warning, the door closed behind me. Cautiously, I went into a room with a sofa: a white sofa brighter than anything in the house. It was like it was calling me. As I tentatively sat on the sofa, I looked at the blank walls on either side of me. Suddenly, the wind started whistling ferociously, lights started flickering. Then the sofa gave way into a large hole right under my legs, which were cut with sharp branches in the forest. Before I knew it, I fell into darkness...

Noor Ali (12)
Heath Park School, Wolverhampton

Trapped

Jessie had won the lottery! 10 million pounds! The first thing she did was rush to her parents' house. Hundreds of questions dancing in her head.

When she arrived; her parents weren't home. Their phones were off. Where were they?

Suddenly, there was a loud scream. She jumped, looking behind her. It was her mom's wedding ring. She could hear her heart beating. She ran to get help.

There were buildings upside down. People walking through one another like ghosts.

Was this real? Why couldn't she open her eyes?

Trapped!

Diya Grewal
Heath Park School, Wolverhampton

Trapped

Trapped. Trapped. Trapped. It's as if my life has been all but a dream. Or has it? Sitting in my room. All alone. In the dark. My head spinning in wonder wondering what to do in life. "Nothing." All I am is trapped. Will I ever get out? My heart drops for a second. I hear something approaching my door. I feel like screaming, but I don't have the power to do it. I sit there waiting and waiting... until blood floods around the door. Memories start rolling in my head. The ones I never wanted to see ever again.

Kristers Belakovs (12)
Heath Park School, Wolverhampton

Trapped

If I had the chance to go back, I would. Every day's become harder but there's nothing I can do about it. After going into the simulation, I had no other choice but to decide whether I should stay or leave. I lived in a world full of hatred and discrimination but I believed that in the other world, there was hope. I can remember having to fight to do what was right, but it was hard. Unfortunately, I didn't listen and it's been the worst moments of my life; I hope you don't make the same decision I made.

Katya Troath (12)
Heath Park School, Wolverhampton

Trapped

It was 9pm, coming back from a party, Will turned into the dark alleyway.

Suddenly, he felt a harsh grasp around his neck, a hood went over his head.

After a short car journey, he was thrown into a cold room with a concrete floor. The only thing he could make out were gleams of light through cracks in the staircase. Will attempted to barge out but he was too weak.

Leaning against the door; a man with a deep voice swung it open. The man had a gun and it was now pointed at Will's head.

"Please!" he screamed...

Gurbinder Ghalli (13)
Heath Park School, Wolverhampton

Trapped

I awake as the burning smell singes my nostrils. I run to the door. Locked! Panicked I run to the window. Locked!
I'm floating. The floor has given way... I groan as a shard of glass embeds itself in my leg. I wipe sweat from my face as I rise to my feet, frantically gripping another door handle. I jump back with a screeching yelp: it's scorching.
I'm trapped. I curl up in a ball; It's over for me.
Eeee! Eeee! My alarm clock jolts me out of my fiery nightmare. I feel a wave of relief wash over me.

Scarlet Bennett (11)
Heath Park School, Wolverhampton

Enclosed In A Cave

Suddenly, I bashed my head against a rock. Some hours later I regained consciousness, my head hurt but I still got up to inspect the scene, wandering around my dark surroundings. The place was dark and I could barely see anything. After feeling around a bit more I realised that I was trapped in a cave. I kept looking around in a panic, searching for any possible exit. I looked up only to see a dot of light poking through the ceiling. Knowing that there was no hope of escape I lay down on the cold floor, accepting my fate.

Vynxnt Jericho Melo (11)
Heath Park School, Wolverhampton

Trapped

On the 23rd June 2019, me and my friends went on a submarine trip. We were planning to go from Brighton to North America, but there was a twist.

When we started to get closer to America there were massive rocks which was unusual. Once we passed a few, unexpectedly a towering rock was in our way and we could not move in time, so we crashed.

We were stranded for years it seemed with hardly any supplies of food or drinks. We were trapped!

Five days later a fellow submarine came and spotted us, we had been reported missing.

Freddie Neale (11)

Heath Park School, Wolverhampton

Trapped

He woke up instantly. Gasping for breath, the man was confused and didn't know where he was. The last thing he remembered was a dark figure hitting him in the head. All he had was a few pieces of food that could only last for a few days. Scared, the man looked around. The walls were stained with dried blood and human skulls were aligned in a mountain. As he looked around, he shuddered at the fact that he was in this monster of a room. He could hardly breathe when he heard silent, quick footsteps. He was not alone...

Sukhdeep Mann
Heath Park School, Wolverhampton

Trapped

Knock! Knock! There was someone at the door, Dad said he would answer it so he went to the door and when he opened it there was a man standing there, with a knife in his hand! Dad turned around and started running, all of a sudden the man chucked the knife and it hit dad's back! Me and Mom ran straight to the to the basement door. Mom opened it and said, "Go in!" Mom followed me in. The killer somehow found where Mom and I were, we were trapped in the basement... Dad jumped and landed on him...

Kayden Hines (11)
Heath Park School, Wolverhampton

Inequality

Eyes burning into my skin, the whispers loud. I knew why and I think everyone who lived in my town knew why. I'm a mixed-race girl trapped in a racist town. I've heard it all before, the racist comments. I can't step out of my house without someone attacking me. I try not to let it hurt, but when you're constantly told you're not good enough, it does. There are days where I love being Jamaican, but then I just want to be like everybody else. My mom says I'm unique, but I can read her too well.

Alannah Miles (12)
Heath Park School, Wolverhampton

Trapped

The building was on fire. I wasn't doing anything to save myself. I was paralysed. My brain and body stopped functioning. There was faint banging on the door, it got louder. The door broke but nobody was behind it. I heard a roar and screamed; nothing came out. I knocked over a bottle of gasoline, which worsened the flames. I was trapped and stood motionless. The fire reached me. Suddenly, I woke up and found that I was surrounded by family members. I smiled while they looked at me concerned.
The dream was over.

Prachi Joshi
Heath Park School, Wolverhampton

Trapped

I was walking in the woods and heard a noise. These woods were abandoned so this was strange. When I turned, I saw a black figure so I decided to explore. I found some large footprints that couldn't be mine, it seemed strange. I suddenly passed out, my thoughts were drowning me. When I woke up I was in some kind of room, my head was spinning. This room had no air; my mouth was taped together; my hands were tied. Everything was silent, then I realised the same black figure I saw earlier that day had trapped me...

Mia Lau (11)
Heath Park School, Wolverhampton

Trapped

I open my eyes, I'm way too exhausted. Wait a minute... I suddenly cannot move, it's not like I don't want to, it's like I'm paralysed. I can't even move my eyes. Is this a coma? I try to open my mouth to scream, but I can't. Oh no... I must move! I must. All of my family think I'm dead. I'm trying to move, but I can't.
A few days have gone by now, and my family truly do believe I am in a coma. I fear that I am that truly stuck here... Forever. I'm forever trapped...

Kaira Lewis
Heath Park School, Wolverhampton

Trapped

He lay there dying to use the lavatory. Carefully he climbed over his wife. He peeped over to see if anybody else was awake, nobody was. As he shut the door the sound of snoring drifted away.

Nobody knew about the man in the restroom. When he was done, he washed his hands and went to leave... the door was stuck he tried shouting, but nobody heard. He was trapped!

Huddling up to himself he began looking around. That's when he saw it so small, so unrecognisable, he grabbed it and unlocked the door, he was free.

Keira Swatman

Heath Park School, Wolverhampton

Trapped

I was walking down this alleyway on my way to the hospital to see my brother, when this ghost-like figure started following me. I wasn't really aware of it at first.
I turned around to see what was there. Nothing. From the corner of my eye I knew there was something following me. The thing eventually caught up to me. It looked like a little boy. He told me that everything was going to be alright and was comforting me. It felt nice to be comforted. The ghost looked a lot like my brother. It was my brother...

Lania Salah (13)
Heath Park School, Wolverhampton

The Day That Would Never End

I was running, darkness chased me as the sky looked like a pool of blood. Back then, I didn't have time to think about that as my instincts were on running and escaping. As I ran I saw a light. I ran into it as I thought it was home. I scanned the area, it was daytime, normal people were walking around instead of gushing blood everywhere; something felt off, the sky turned red and all I could feel behind was darkness. It caught me, I was trapped. I woke up again and realised I was in a reoccurring world.

Darrell Nyamunda (12)

Heath Park School, Wolverhampton

Trapped

I woke up to loud screaming it was my mom I ran downstairs and saw a trail of blood. I heard screaming again, it was my dad. I ran upstairs to wake up my sisters up, they were not there, only blood. I had almost peed myself by then, I couldn't see anyone, at first I thought it was a prank, but then I saw my sister's body, I was crying and screaming. I then heard an unfamiliar voice saying. "Shut up!" I went downstairs, picked up my knife and followed the trail to the door it was locked...

Tanish Kaushal
Heath Park School, Wolverhampton

I'm Trapped

At first it was okay. The voice would direct me and give me little tasks that would help me. It was soothing, like a mother with her child. It befriended me and I soon grew accustomed to its behaviours. I was bewitched, and I would sometimes do things I didn't want to do.
It changed. I am now standing at a house. In my hand is a bat. I want to run away, but I'm driven forward. It's the middle of the night and he is in control. He tells me do the inevitable. I can't resist.
I'm trapped.

Haya Rhuma
Heath Park School, Wolverhampton

Trapped

I woke up, body hurting, how did I get here? It was a bit dark. I shouted. I saw him through the window, his van stopped. The driver got out. I got claustrophobic. The doors shook, he was trying to get in so I sat down and held my legs tight. The door wouldn't open. In the distance I heard sirens. Through the little window I saw the man running. I heard the police and once again I shouted. I waited, then the van shook, a dog burst in. I saw police cars and a crowd. I wasn't trapped anymore.

Ryan Hawkins (12)
Heath Park School, Wolverhampton

Trapped

I'm stuck, I'm lost and my mind is going crazy, I don't know where I am. Chains are on my hands. I rip the chains off, I wander around. I look around and I find the door, it's locked, it's made out of something metal. I find the key and escape. Now I'm free, well that's what I thought. I see a man dressed all black with a mask so I run. I am hiding in a cupboard. He laughs and finds me, he grabs me by the neck and throws me in the room, and now I'm trapped forever...

Paula Reinfelde

Heath Park School, Wolverhampton

Trapped

Trapped on an island alone. Nothing but a few trees. The only thing that kept me company were the birds. Most of them were nice.

I was tired a lot of the time. On the first night I looked for food but only found more sand.

Every night kept on getting shorter, it rained most nights, so I had to make a shelter which took a while to build. One of the nights I thought I might die because the shelter was about to collapse.

The shelter stayed strong, but I didn't sleep. I wish I could just get home.

Lilly Goodwin
Heath Park School, Wolverhampton

Trapped

I have always been different. As a child I never played with action figures or toy cars. It's always been Barbies or make-up, this is how I have been from a young age. I've always been told to act like a man. At times I feel trapped; trapped in someone I don't want to be.

Even when I go to school, I always feel like there are groups of people judging me for who I am. I think to myself, *do I even have friends and family who love me for me?* When I think about it, I'm alone.

Esha Bhakar
Heath Park School, Wolverhampton

Trapped In The Unthinkable

Waking up in a dark spruce box was not one thing I asked Santa for, yet he decided to give me Christmas three months early.

I feel like a rare animal being held hostage by poachers; I don't know where I am, rocking side to side I'm pretty sure I'm amongst a boat; on sea or somewhere else but I honestly do not know. Being that type of kid who is curious and likes to discover, I start to feel the box, feeling my surroundings, looking for something that will trigger my escape route...

Shadi Damree (11)
Heath Park School, Wolverhampton

Trial Of Dreams

I'm awake, where am I? A voice called out, "To gain your freedom you must face 3 challenges, walk through the door." The first challenge was parkour, I started the parkour and now I had reached the second door. There was a puzzle next to me, I had completed the puzzle, platforms appeared for me to jump on, now I reached the final door. All I saw was a bed. I thought I should go to sleep and clear my mind. I woke up, I was at the place I got attacked at. It was a dream, or was it?

Rares Ignatescu
Heath Park School, Wolverhampton

Trapped

3... 2... 1... I took a breath, surrounded by water. My leg was trapped; I couldn't see anything. Tugging at my leg, I tried to break free but it wasn't working. I remembered something: the jack. I reached for it, inches away. I finally managed to grab it and wedge it under my leg. I was running out of air fast. I tried to open one of the doors but it was no use; the car was fully submerged now. There was no way out, the windows, doors, boot, nothing. It was no use. I was trapped...

Georgina Corbett (12)
Heath Park School, Wolverhampton

The Mission

I was in a train in someone's body. There was a minute timer. *Boom!* An explosion occurred. I appeared somewhere and a note said: 'Defuse the bomb.

I didn't find the bomb. It felt like I was trapped in an infinite loop of time. I found a key and I used it, then the bomb exploded.

I found it and used it, there it was and I tried to defuse it until I cut the wrong wire and blew up.

I got the key found the bomb and I cut the correct wires. Then I did another mission...

Josh Butler (11)
Heath Park School, Wolverhampton

Trapped

Who? What? Where?

Lay down, splayed out on an oak floor in what looked like a large room. There was no way in and no way out.

In the centre of the room, sat a small piece of white paper. Slowly, she made her way towards it, being careful not to move too clumsily towards what could be a trap. Reaching for it, the scared girl realised that it was not a piece of paper at all but a piece of cloth dripping with red blood-like ink inscrolled with two words... 'You're trapped!'

Leah Blakemore

Heath Park School, Wolverhampton

Trapped In A Deep Dark Place

I woke up, I knew I was trapped footsteps were approaching me, the person bust down the door. I saw a silhouette he seemed as if he had a weapon in his hand but I thought I was hallucinating because I'd had a hit on the head. He came closer he had a knife in his hand. I begged for mercy, he seemed like he didn't care. He came closer... that was no face that was a hockey mask. He lifted the knife then a man saved me by grabbing the knife off him and stabbing him in the chest.

Kieran
Heath Park School, Wolverhampton

Trapped In My Dream

Out of nowhere where I had woken up, my head was aching. It felt as if I was beaten up and thrown in this dark room. I felt my way around the place and I was shocked, shocked to see that there was an endless loop of darkness. I felt very light-headed and I collapsed onto the floor. When I woke up, the place was familiar; it was my home and my family were standing around me. In shock they told me that I was screaming and shouting and it seemed as if it was trapped in my own dream.

Mohamed Amin-Mahamed (11)
Heath Park School, Wolverhampton

Trapped

I heard banging and the sound of the TV, so I ran down the stairs, but the TV was off. I dashed to the basement where I stayed for several hours. Screams came from the room above when suddenly it was quiet. I ran to the top of the stairs but the door was locked then I remembered I had a bobby pin in my hair. I tried to unlock the door but no luck I was trapped, I was there all night. Not only was I cold, I had no food, no water; I had no chance of survival...

Georgia Knowles (12)
Heath Park School, Wolverhampton

Trapped

Suddenly, I heard the door click behind me, I was trapped in a shop full of sweets. From the corner of my eye, I saw a lever - I didn't know whether to pull it or not.
I pulled it.
Hovering over my head was a tube, it covered my body and slowly began to move downwards. When it opened, I was amazed.
I looked around and saw sugar everywhere it was a dream come true. I saw a key and climbed back into the tube; I was back in the shop. It had worked.

Omed Hamid Hassan (11)
Heath Park School, Wolverhampton

Trapped

Light shone on the man who was slumped over and tied up in the icy metal chair. In the shadows sat a giant pale man with an angry stare looking at the peaceful sleeping man. His legs were bandaged, and bloodstained.
Slowly, his eyes flickered open and terror filled them. To his left, he saw a young girl, pale as a ghost lying lifeless on the cold stone floor beside a bloodstained mattress.

Davina Thomas
Heath Park School, Wolverhampton

Trapped

Silence. The room was dark and cold, I was confused. A tremor of fear shot through my spine, I didn't know where I was or what I could do.
I peered round the gloomy hallway...
A black silhouette, lurking in the shadows, I was terrified. I slammed myself against the ground, trembling and shaking with fear. *Bang!*
I knew I was next.

William Robinson (13)
Heath Park School, Wolverhampton

Punishment

We are watching, we always are, from the inside not living life. Looking through eyes that aren't mine, talking through a mouth that isn't mine. Living a life that isn't mine. I have scales, sharp teeth and blood on my hands. Hence, I'm a demon with a gift - a soul.

"How dare you, you are my punishment and I am yours. You have no scales, sharp teeth or blood on your hands. Try having a soul diluting your heart."

"You try having an evil shell."

The irony, we're trapped together and the only way out is to die!

Holly Hopkinson (11)
Kirk Balk Academy, Hoyland

Trapped

I can't. I can't move. Not my hands, not my feet. Not even my head side to side. I'm trapped. The feeling is indescribable. The edges of the spiked, dreaded box edge closer towards me. It makes me scream but the thick metal walls make my scream unknown to the outside. I feel unbelievably scared. I have a fear of the unknown and right now everything is the unknown. Where I am, who has done this and why I am here. Fear watches over me like a predator watching its prey. Then I think I know, it's the-Argh!

Lucy Armer (11)
Kirk Balk Academy, Hoyland

Move On

Only 30 seconds until the bell would go. I walked out the door, when Logan Moore dragged me to the PE room. "Loser, give my money or else!" I gave him the money, shaking. He beat me up anyway, I couldn't move. My mind began to come up with these horrible theories. I'm trapped. No one will help me. Nobody cares about me. I couldn't feel my body on the cold dusty floor. As the door closed, I shut my eyes as a tear of pain shed. A bone was broken. Or was I just broken?

Olivia Haigh (11)
Kirk Balk Academy, Hoyland

Shattered Glass

The sharp glass shards pierced through the brittle flesh of my arm. I was alone in a dark room, hardly able to see my hands in front of my face. The glass wall began to fix itself. Quickly, I dashed to the wall, hoping with everything I had left that I could make it to the mortal world again. It moved, the glass wall kept retreating backwards, just beyond my reach. There was no escape, it was healed, I was never getting out. I was going to be here for eternity or at least as long as I'd be alive.

Oliver Hancock (11)
Minsthorpe Community College, South Elmsall

Darkness

My heart began to race with sweat slowly dripping from the tips of my fingers. Where did I lie, or should I say, where did my body lie? Trying to scream for help as I was plummeted back into silence. My body lay still unable to move, my mind carried on racing. Pushing myself to wake up but no matter how hard I tried I was still stuck. I could hear footsteps coming towards me. I began panicking, searching with all my might to find a way out. Why did I have to suffer the trauma of this horrific coma?

Tegan Gladys Lynne Patton (13)
Minsthorpe Community College, South Elmsall

Trapped

Trapped. Trapped in an unfortunate suffocating sphere of outdated stereotypes, kindly gifted in response to our race, gender, ethnicity or sexuality. Trapped in a society of hatred whereby a crime glides hastily over our minds - unsurprising and unquestioned. Trapped on a planet painted with unrequited love, screaming helplessly for hydration, structure and normality. Trapped behind rose-tinted glasses, enclosed in unanswered questions, incomplete answers, false truths, hurtful lies. Trapped in a concealed society sparsely scattered with entrances, coated completely in padlocked exits. Trapped in consented violence, united in isolation, enclosed in a deafening silence. Trapped with inexistent optimism of escaping.

Lucy Evans (17)
St George's School, Harpenden

Trapped

I desperately scrambled through the rusty, decayed mailbox for the newspaper buried somewhere amongst my overdue bills. Finally, I felt the scrunched paper against my weathered hands. 21st May, 2006 read the front page in italic writing. No, this couldn't be happening, could it? Anxiety consumed me, devouring every ounce of happiness I had left. Standing outside the front door like a rabbit in the headlights, my body drained of hope, as I realised it was the day of my best friend's death, which I was responsible for. I was reliving the day repeatedly. Trapped in my own personal hell.

Olivia McPhillips (12)
St George's School, Harpenden

Blue Lights

Bang! went the ricochet of a bullet on its crash-course mission to my leg. I didn't want to stop, to succumb to the darkness, my inadequacies, my failures. But with every second I could feel the conviction oozing from my body. With my last shred of will, I trudged onwards like a thief in the night. With every agonising step away from the deafening sirens, I came closer to freedom's door, further from the blue lights flashing relentlessly through the streets. I turned the corner and there they were, dressed in blue... There was no escape. I was trapped.

Catherine Kola-Balogun (15)
St George's School, Harpenden

Trapped

My head swung left and right searching for an exit. Cautiously, I swerved round a sharp corner in the gargantuan maze that would prise my bones forever, it seemed. My ear-piercing screams were drowned out by the howling of wolves in the midnight moon. Vines crept up the elongated walls of solid brick around me whilst sweat trickled down my cheeks. As I sprinted in every direction, seeking safety, I tripped over a wooden root covered in razor-sharp ivy. My knees crunched the ground as I collapsed, screaming into the night air. Was I going to make it out?

Max Soothill (11)
St George's School, Harpenden

Trapped

Silence surrounded me like the glaze of the night sky. The rapid pounding of my heart caused my breathing to hasten. What is happening? I gazed depressingly at the red strips of my body, and I instantly knew. The pressuring eyes of millions of people stared at me intensely. I had to get away, to stop this, I had to try. Struggling, I sprinted blindly through the darkness until light emerged. I took my last chance and ran closer. Strangely, as I entered the beam, a wave of relief filled me. I was finally happy, and I was finally free.

Jasmine Lota (13)
St George's School, Harpenden

Trapped

Out of the corner of my eye I see him moving slowly as he sleeps. I think that on the whole he has dealt with it all very well. If I had gone through what he has, I don't know if I would have been able to struggle through like he did. He is a true soldier - always fighting. But now I have him cornered. He is vulnerable. There is no open window of opportunity for him now. Poor soul - it isn't really his fault. Hush now, he's about to awake. I watch him as he realises, he's trapped.

Alexander Russell (14)
St George's School, Harpenden

Trapped

The human mind can be a struggle to control. Most can wield its power, but some cannot. Some are trapped in their own heads, slaves to their thoughts. Escape is a difficult thing to grasp, escape keeps slipping out of their fingers and leaving them to suffer. Escape taunts them from afar. It watches them struggle, mockingly.

Alex Falconer (13)
St George's School, Harpenden

YOUNG WRITERS INFORMATION

We hope you have enjoyed reading this book – and that you will continue to in the coming years.

If you're a young writer who enjoys reading and creative writing, or the parent of an enthusiastic poet or story writer, do visit our website **www.youngwriters.co.uk**. Here you will find free competitions, workshops and games, as well as recommended reads, a poetry glossary and our blog. There's lots to keep budding writers motivated to write!

If you would like to order further copies of this book, or any of our other titles, then please give us a call or order via your online account.

Young Writers
Remus House
Coltsfoot Drive
Peterborough
PE2 9BF
(01733) 890066
info@youngwriters.co.uk